WILD MATE

MATEMATCH OUTCASTS BOOK 6

ARIANA HAWKES

Imprint: Independently published

ISBN: 9798682727629

www.arianahawkes.com

CHAPTER 1

Dana

The whole world was being destroyed.

The apocalypse had finally come.

Dana's bed rocked and juddered like a tiny boat on a stormy ocean, while from all sides terrible growls and howls assailed her ears.

Her eyes flew open. She was in her RV, and the dim light of dawn was filtering through the curtains. Her heart beat slowed a little.

Woah, that was some trippy dream—

she started to tell herself.

No, not a dream. Because the noise and shaking hadn't stopped. Her heart sped up again and panic gripped her throat. A dream about a boat capsizing on a turbulent sea at least made some kind of sense. But the RV tossing about like it was being flipped over—

The feral sounds continued, getting louder. She opened her mouth to scream but a terrible screech ripped from one end of the vehicle to the other, stealing her breath.

That was claws. Definitely long, sharp claws. And they were trying to rip her out of there like a sardine from a can.

She struggled up from her bunk, but the rocking threw her back down again. As she jolted against the mattress a gasp blasted through her throat and finally, she had her voice back.

"Skylar!" she screamed, as loud as she could. The sound rang through the small space as if it were an echo chamber and Dana's friend's head rose up from a nearby pile of pillows.

"What the—holy hell!" Skylar's voice was rough from sleep. Somehow she'd slept through the first part of the attack.

If that's what it was.

"What's happening?" Skylar groaned, still not as close to screaming as Dana.

Dana opened her mouth to answer, but something very hard and heavy hit the side of the van, and it slammed up on two wheels. Dana wailed as she was thrown against the side wall. A low snorting sound came from somewhere nearby. She grabbed a blanket and pulled it over her head, burrowing down as if she were a rabbit that could save itself if only it could dig deep enough. Skylar had given up on trying to speak and was howling like a scared animal instead.

"It's going to stop, it's going to stop," Dana muttered to herself, keeping her head down and her eyes closed. There was no such thing as monsters. That was a fact, wasn't it? No matter how scary it was, those things out there wouldn't tear into the RV and eat them… Would they?

A louder, deeper roar shattered through the other frightening sounds. It was so shocking that they both yelped and Skylar hurtled into Dana's bed. They found each other in the mess of bedding, gripping each other's hands. Dana cowered against her friend, listening to the growling and scuffling going on outside.

The massive roar sounded again and again as the other sounds faded. There was a sound of feet scuttling across damp earth, then everything became still.

The girls clung to each other, waiting to see if they were safe or if they had traded one danger for another.

"Hello?" A gruff voice spoke outside. "Is someone in there?"

"Yes!" Skylar squeaked. "Are we safe now?"

There was a pause. "Yes you are. For now."

Dana was so relieved to hear a human voice that she leapt up and ran to the door. As she flung it open, she was expecting to be greeted by a policeman, a ranger, maybe a kindly old woodsman.

But she went rigid in the doorway, trapping Skylar behind her. It was a man alright, but not the comforting type she had been hoping for. He was tall, rough and unkempt. When his eyes—one blue and the other startlingly black— flashed over her, it was like he was looking right through to her bones.

Her mouth fell open but no words came out. The silence stretched around them for a few seconds until Skylar pushed her way past and hurried down the stairs, arms outstretched as if she was planning on hugging the man.

"Skylar!" Dana hissed.

But Skylar was unabashed. "You saved us!" she exclaimed.

The man's face stiffened and he took two steps away. Dana crept down the stairs, too, not sure if she was looking for comfort from Skylar or if she wanted to try and protect her from this strange, dangerous-looking man.

"You were lucky I was here," he said, gruffly. "This is no place for unaccompanied humans."

Skylar folded her arms and stuck her chin out. "It's a free country," she said.

Dana groaned. Challenge to Skylar was like a red rag to a bull.

The man's massive head swung from side to side. "Ragtown is not a free country," he said, each word enunciated slowly in a deep snarly tone that sent shivers through her.

"Ragtown?" Dana whispered. The word was familiar, but she wasn't sure where she'd heard it before. "Where are we?"

The man looked over Skylar's shoulder at her, his face softening just a little. "I mean it, ladies. You need to get out of town. This is a stupid place to camp."

"Are you calling me stupid?" Skylar planted her hands on her hips.

"I am if you decided to camp here." He frowned. "What the hell are you two doing here?" He looked over Skylar's shoulder at Dana again, and since he seemed to be addressing her, she tried to find her voice.

"We were—are, on a road trip. Exploring, enjoying the freedom of the open road..."

The man looked as if that made no sense to him at all. "But how did you end up here? It's not somewhere you find by chance."

"Um." Skylar looked at the ground, rubbing her arm. "Dana," she mumbled over her shoulder, "I didn't want to tell you because I thought you might freak out."

Dana's fear melted away as she sprung in front of Skylar and glared at her.

"Tell me what?"

"Don't freak out."

"What have you done?"

"I drove us to a shifter town."

"What!?"

"I said don't freak out!"

"And I never promised I wouldn't! What the hell are you doing to me, Skylar?"

Skylar's lip trembled, just a little. "Dana, you know I have my reasons—"

"And I have my reasons!" Her voice was thick with fury as she stepped towards her friend. Skylar squared up as well, but the man coughed deliberately.

"It seems you ladies have a lot to talk about, so I'll leave you to it," he said, his face wrought with confusion and dismay. "Just remember what I said and get out of town. I don't expect to see you here when I get back."

"Oh, we will, don't worry," Dana called at his retreating back. She turned back to Skylar, cursing herself for having fallen asleep in the back of the RV last night while Skylar was still driving. She jabbed her index finger in her friend's face as if it were a loaded weapon.

"Skylar, how could you have brought us here? You know how I feel about shifters. And you could have gotten us killed! Who knows what would've happened if that guy hadn't come along!"

"Dana, I'm sorry—" Skylar began in a wheedling voice.

"Well, you don't look sorry. You look like you got away with something." Dana paced back and forth, trying to get her emotions under control. "My own mother abandoned us to be with a shifter. You know this! They're feral. Unprincipled. I can't even stand the thought of them—"

"And you know why I need a shifter." Skylar caught

5

Dana's elbow. "I need to find one who can give me a baby. A strong one that I won't lose."

Dana shook her head in disgust. "You're saying you're planning to spend the rest of your life in this dump of a town, while trying not to get eaten?"

Skylar blinked. "No. I just want a baby daddy. Then we're getting the hell out of Ragtown. Believe me, this place is already giving me the creeps."

"So, what, you're going to hang around bars or something, until some animal throws you over his shoulder and drags you home to his lair? That's very classy, Sky."

"Please Dana, I just want to find a guy, get pregnant and leave. That's all. You don't understand how much I want a baby."

Dana looked at her friend, whose eyes were now filled with tears. It was true that she'd never grasped Skylar's overwhelming passion to have a child at any cost. But it was real. She'd experienced Skylar's distress and comforted her so many times.

Dana didn't want to be here, not at all. But she knew that if this one thing could give Skylar what she needed, then she had to give it a chance.

She puffed out her cheeks. "Okay. But we can't go wandering around here. We need a plan. Need to think outside the box."

Skylar beamed at Dana, glad to have her friend's support. "I already did that. Come on, let's park the van around there and we can go get breakfast in that café."

Dana climbed back into the RV and Skylar jumped into the driver's seat, before pulling the big vehicle around to park around the corner from a cute little café on Main Street. Dana had to admit, for such a rough town, it had a very nice-looking coffee shop.

The building across the street also looked bright and welcoming—a little pizza parlor. She wasn't planning to enjoy her stay here, but at least it might not be complete torture. Surely, some decent people must live here if there were such nice, homely places.

Skylar dragged Dana into the café and straight up to the counter. A curvy woman with bright, wavy red hair adjusted her red rimmed glasses and eyed them skeptically.

"Hello." Skylar bulldozed right into the conversation, obliterating tact as she so often did. "You're Florence, aren't you? I need to know why you haven't responded to my messages." She slapped the counter for effect.

"Messages?" Dana echoed.

Florence took a breath, her curvy bosom making a movement all its own as she looked the two girls over.

"Skylar, I assume?" Florence did not sound impressed.

"Yes! You know me. You should. I've sent dozens of applications. Why haven't you responded to me?"

Florence's eyes narrowed as she looked right into Skylar's face. Dana had the sudden impression of a fluffy-tailed squirrel hiding his favorite nut from the rest of the population.

"There is no mate for you here. Not with that attitude." Florence's tone was final.

"Excuse me?" Nothing was final to Skylar. "What attitude? What are you talking about?"

"Just as I said. There is no mate for you in this town. You can send me as many applications as you want. There is no match." She looked past Skylar and met Dana's eye. Dana smiled nervously, wondering why she was getting the woman's attention.

"Your friend, however, she might have a match."

"What?" Both Dana and Skylar exclaimed at the same time.

"How can she have a match when I don't!" Skylar yelled.

"How can I even have a match when I don't want one?" Dana yelled back.

Florence shrugged, looking them over. "It is how it is. I don't make the rules."

"You can't match me without my consent," Dana insisted, but Florence raised her hands helplessly, as if it was the will of the universe and completely out of her control.

"No," Dana said loudly. "Not happening. I hate shif—" She broke off, looking Florence up and down. Maybe it was no *coincidence* that the woman looked like a squirrel. She'd better not insult her entire species.

Instead, she turned and stormed out in disgust. She was ready to walk out on the whole town and Skylar's stupid plan. She strode along Main Street in the direction of the RV, Skylar's plaintive voice following her all the way.

CHAPTER 2

Timon

The door of the pizza parlor swung open to admit two customers and Piper called,
"Hi! Welcome to Timon's!"

Timon shook his head at the way her loud, excited voice cut through the sound of the lunchtime rush. No one else seemed to mind much though, as Piper's bright smile and enthusiastic manner were hard to resist. But he was a quiet bear and his sister's lively presence was taking a lot of getting used to.

His sister.

Timon was still struggling with the idea that he had a sister. For as long as he could remember, he had been alone. He was strange—even to other shifters. Awkward. A loner. And he had always carried a certainty that he would never be accepted by anyone. Yes, he'd found a home in Ragtown—

that sanctuary for broken souls, where everyone had a jagged-edged past that tore at their dreams and threatened to overwhelm their days. But even here he'd felt like the odd man out.

Until Piper had arrived, bursting with positivity and enthusiasm to meet her big brother.

Timon moved to the main counter with a big handful of dough. He slapped it down on the floured bench and worked it with his hands, swirling it until the elasticity tugged it back together. Then he picked it up again, twisted it, and tossed it back down.

"You are really good at that." Piper reached for another slice of cheese and pepperoni he'd put out to snack on.

He gave her a sideways glance. "You got worms or something?"

"What?" She let out a screech of laughter.

"That's the second pizza you've eaten this morning, and you're hardly any bigger than my arm."

She shrugged. "A bear's gotta eat."

He grinned. "Guess you are my sister after all," he said and a twinge of affection hit him right in the chest. Already he felt a familiarity with her that he'd never felt before, with anyone. It was a strange feeling, but welcome.

"Still don't believe me?" She chewed thoughtfully, golden-brown eyes glinting under the lights. "You could always fight me again, just to check." She wiggled her eyebrows humorously and grinned, but deep inside him, his bear yowled with shame.

She laughed. "Settle down there, big fella. I wasn't serious."

"Neither was I." He focused on pummeling the dough. "It's not like I attacked you for real. I just needed to shift to see if you were telling the truth."

Piper laughed easily. "And kick my ass, if it came to that?"

"Well, look. I never said I was going to kick anyone's ass—"

"Oh, stop it. You were challenging me with all your mighty bear strength. If we weren't related, then my bear would have torn into you and we'd both be in a few pieces now."

Timon smiled, trying to make light of the situation, as she was doing. In truth, he'd been disturbed by the encounter. For a man who had never had family, having a sister suddenly appear out of nowhere was about as scary as life got.

He had challenged her with everything he had. He had been fully prepared to run off that crazy bear who'd dared to say she was his sister. Then feeling his bear back down, knowing that the scent flooding his nostrils was part of him —these things had disturbed Timon greatly.

He'd even tried to stir his rage up, thinking that it was so impossible he had family that it had to be some kind of trick. But his bear simply refused to rise. There was no challenge there. From that moment on, the hard part had been accepting that he was no longer completely alone...and trying to get to know his new sister.

Timon really wasn't good with people. Opening the pizza shop had been a massive step for him and he was making progress towards being approachable—maybe even friendly. That still didn't mean he had any clue about how to behave around a sibling.

Piper had made it easy for him. Over the four weeks she'd been in town, she had done more than put him at ease. She had drawn him out, gotten him talking about his past and his hopes for the future. But the one thing that bugged him was that she never answered his questions about where she'd come from, or where the rest of the family was.

Sometimes she dodged the questions altogether; other times she told him it would all come out in time. He knew she was keeping things from him, but he trusted her to tell him when she was ready. Trust was a strange sensation for Timon, and he doubted he could have learned it at all if it wasn't for Piper.

Just as Timon was pressing his rolling pin into a big pile of dough, the lights flickered and went out.

"What the—?" Piper exclaimed, and a bunch of gruff, dismayed cries rang around the room. Timon cursed as he rushed out the back to the fuse box. This was the third weird incident in as many days. One of the kitchen pipes had busted, flooding the kitchen. The oven's grate had gotten blocked unexpectedly, filling the oven with soot.

And now this.

He grumbled to himself as he flipped the switches. This time of year was just bad luck. Usually, he liked to hibernate through the winters. The coldest season always brought dark thoughts and fits of bad mood he just couldn't shake, and he was plagued by nightmares and feelings of déjà vu. Hibernating usually blanked it out completely—a rest far deeper than sleep and dreams.

And with every day that more bad luck piled up, he again regretted his decision to stay awake this year.

With a bit of tinkering Timon got the lights back up, noticing that some wires had frayed apart, exactly like they had a few days ago. Soon he was going to have to rip out the whole system and replace it. From the main room, Piper gave a whoop of delight, and there were claps and cheers of appreciation from the customers.

Timon strode back into the restaurant in relief, but then he stopped dead, unable to believe what he was seeing.

The two women from this morning! The utter fools who'd thought that camping in the thick of a town full of social rejects was a great idea. When they approached the counter, he couldn't keep the scowl off his face.

Automatically, his gaze fell on the small one, the one with the shiny black hair and the bright green eyes that scanned him watchfully. *Dana.* That was her name. It burst into his mind like the flutter of a butterfly's wings. Her lips were pursed in a taut line and she looked scared. He didn't blame her.

"Hi, Timon!" the other one—*Skylar, was it?*—greeted him with a breezy smile.

"I told you two to get out," he grunted.

Her face fell, just a little. She recovered quickly and gave him a sassy smile.

"We *are.* God, you Ragtown people are so *sensitive.*" She rolled her eyes. "I'm just working on my match, then we'll be out of here."

"Don't wait for that," he barked, hurling the ball of pizza dough on the counter. "Just go. Bad things can happen to humans in this town."

"Tell me about it," Dana muttered, hugging herself. "I've had enough already."

Timon frowned, trying not to notice how her green eyes sparkled beneath her thick bangs. He liked the way she had her hair, in a short bob. It made her look cute and mischievous.

He shook himself mentally. It didn't matter how cute she was. He shouldn't be noticing things like that, anyway.

"So, Timon—" Skylar planted herself on a stool right next to Piper, who was watching the scene with unconcealed interest. "Dish me the goss. Who's single in this town? Is there anyone looking for a mate?"

Timon tried to focus on his dough again. "There's plenty of guys around looking for a pretty girl like you," he grunted. "Don't mean it's a good idea."

"But you're a nice guy, right? You saved us from the beasts, and you know how to make pizza. You must have friends. Hook a girl up, can't ya?"

He sensed rather than saw that she was batting her false eyelashes at him. He stopped kneading the dough to stare right into her eyes, certain this was some kind of joke. But when she continued to smile at him eagerly, he realized she was serious.

He shook his head firmly. "You don't know what you're asking."

"Yeah," Piper cut in, laughing. "You haven't spent much time with shifters, have you?"

"Well, hey." Skylar turned to Piper, scowling. "I'm here trying to fix that, but you guys seem bent on making it hard for me."

"Oh, just hang around." Piper took a swallow of soda. "Plenty of guys will introduce themselves, I'm sure."

"Really?" Skylar perked up at the prospect.

"Yeah. Just like they did this morning, right?" Piper's voice was laced with sarcasm.

Dana let out a miserable sigh and gazed out of the restaurant's window as if she was desperate to escape. Timon found himself wishing he could pick her up and carry her away from this ridiculous situation.

Skylar looked just a little bashful. "Well, yeah… But they aren't all like that, are they?" she said plaintively.

Piper put her drink back on the counter. "You're in Ragtown now, honey." She fixed Skylar with a serious expression. "If they aren't all like that, then they're probably worse."

"Piper," Timon cut in. "Have you met Dana?"

"Uh, not really?" Piper looked at him quizzically, no doubt wondering why he felt the need to introduce the girl. The truth was, he wasn't sure himself. He guessed he didn't like the way she was being left out of the conversation, especially when she seemed a hell of a lot smarter than her friend.

"Hi there." Piper waved, and Dana waved back sheepishly.

"Don't worry, we're leaving," Dana said, then she grabbed Skylar's hand. "Skylar, you heard what she said. Let's get out of here—" she broke off, as the door opened again and Jagger, the town sheriff stormed in.

Timon greeted him with some relief.

"There you are." Jagger walked straight up to Dana and Skylar. "I'm the sheriff here. Name's Jagger. I've heard about you two ladies—Dana and Skylar, is it?"

"Yes. That's us." Skylar pouted, instinctively knowing that she was in trouble.

"Look, you can't just move in here." Jagger planted his hands on his hips, emphasizing his huge bulk. "This is a shifter town and it isn't safe for humans. I need you to go."

"Believe me, I'm trying." Dana's voice was low but plaintive.

Skylar shot her an exasperated look. "I only need a few days. You can give me that, can't you? You said you would."

"I don't know, Skylar. The more time goes by, the less I want to stay."

"But—"

"The sheriff just asked us to go. The guy in charge. Doesn't that tell you something?"

"It tells me we need a safe place to stay." Skylar stuck out her bottom lip. Silence hung over the circle and eyes were cast down as if there was no chance of finding what Skylar needed—in any capacity.

"What about the goldmine?" Timon spoke up suddenly. "They could camp there for a couple of days, couldn't they?"

All four of them looked at Timon with disbelief, while he blinked, surprised at his own words.

"They could," Jagger said, nostrils flaring as he exhaled. He turned back to the women. "Just be careful, and don't plan on staying long. I wouldn't want anything to happen to a nice pair of girls like you." He turned around and headed for the door.

Dana leaned on the counter, shaking her head. "Well, that was comforting," she muttered, her tone implying there was no comfort in this situation—or in the town—at all.

CHAPTER 3

Dana

$\mathcal{A}$fter they returned to the RV, Dana took her seat next to Skylar but stared out of the window in silence. Her annoyance at Skylar was growing. They had received enough warnings by now that it should be obvious to her that they weren't welcome in Ragtown.

Welcome or not, it certainly wasn't a place Dana intended to stay. And it had looked like they had their ticket out of there when that Timon guy suddenly suggested the goldmine.

Does he want us to go, or not?

Dana would have sworn from the first meeting that Timon certainly didn't want them hanging around. Why he had suddenly come up with a place for them to camp that might be semi-safe, she couldn't figure.

He sure is cute though.

Dana hushed her mischievous inner voice. It made no difference at all how intriguing those different-colored eyes of his were. He was a shifter. She would be staying far away from him and hopefully, this whole town.

They barely talked on the drive up, Skylar shooting Dana concerned looks as she maneuvered the big van around the turns. After Skylar took a corner so sharply that she almost turned the van right over, Dana finally threw up her hands in exasperation.

"Okay, okay, don't crash the damned RV trying to figure out what I'm thinking. I'll talk to you."

Skylar still looked hesitant and Dana could tell by her face that what was on her mind wasn't a light conversation.

Skylar loved children and couldn't wait to have her own. The miscarriage she'd had with her ex had almost destroyed her. Then she heard of women who'd had trouble conceiving with humans going on to have healthy babies with shifters.

After that, her interest in shifters had become almost an obsession.

Dana had her own feelings about the situation though, and they were as strong as Skylar's, even if they were the polar opposite.

"I know you don't want to be here…" Skylar started.

"Do you?" Dana didn't move, keeping her arms crossed tightly to stop herself from gesturing. "Do you really get it, Skylar?"

"I do, I think I do."

"Can you possibly understand what it's like to have your happy family broken up because your mom fell in love with a shifter and decided he was more important than everything —including her own children?"

"Dana—"

"No. You listen to me. Being here makes my skin crawl, okay? If you were really my friend, you wouldn't have tricked me into coming here, and you would understand how hard it is for me to stay here!"

Skylar gripped the wheel of the RV as she navigated a turn. "Just one more day. Please." Skylar's voice was so low Dana almost couldn't hear it. But she could feel her friend's desperation, her hope. She really believed that this course of action could give her the child she wanted so badly.

Dana sighed. She felt bad for her friend. And she didn't want to be the one to destroy her hopes by forcing her to leave.

"Alright. I can handle that. One more day."

"Thank you!" Skylar took her eyes away from the road just once, to smile at her. "Thank you so much, Dana. You're the best."

Dana sighed. "Just don't make me regret it, okay."

Skylar perked up instantly. "Hey, by the way, I have something I've been meaning to ask you."

"Go ahead." Dana waited for a life-altering question.

"What's your favorite flavor of jellybean?"

"Huh?"

"Do you think the flavor tastes different to the color? Like, even though the red one is raspberry maybe it tastes more like lemonade?"

"Skylar. What the hell are you talking about?"

"You don't have a preference, then?"

"I do like red ones, and they taste just like raspberries to me." Dana threw up her hands helplessly.

This the moment that Skylar goes out of her mind, and I'm going to get dragged along for the ride.

"If you could plant roses or kale, which would you choose and why?"

"Skylar, I've never been near a garden in my life. I hate to get my hands dirty like that."

"But, what would you have in your garden? I'm just curious."

Dana looked at her friend sideways, glad that Skylar had her eyes on the road and wasn't paying attention to her. The face Dana was making would surely have offended her.

"I don't know. Roses are pretty, but kale is really good for you... I don't know enough about gardening to answer the question."

"It doesn't matter—" Skylar looked over, ready to hit Dana with more questions, but seeing her friend's face seemed to stop her in her tracks. "Okay, cool. I'll shut up. It was just a dumb internet survey thing."

"Stay away from those," Dana said absently. "They'll rot your brain."

Skylar turned one final corner and the goldmine came into view. A yawning chasm had been cut into the reddish brown soil, and supported with thick beams of dark wood. Trees surrounded it, rustling in the slight breeze, while above and beyond that, the mountain range reached even higher.

They parked up in a flat area that caught the afternoon sun. The air was warm, and the mountain scenery was quite beautiful. Dana couldn't fault it for a camp site.

When they were set up, Dana called Timon to see if he could give them a ride back to town. She walked some distance away, so Skylar wouldn't hear.

She took a deep breath as she hit dial, trying to convince herself that Skylar was her motivation for doing this.

It had nothing to do with seeing Timon again. No way.

"Hello?" It was the usual way to answer the phone, but Timon sounded more surprised than a person should be in the times of caller I.D.

"Hey! Timon. It's Dana." Her cheeks warmed. She'd felt she had to introduce herself because he'd sounded so surprised, but now she was embarrassed. She cleared her throat.

"I was wondering if you might come up and drive us into town? The camper is all set up and I don't really want to move it so..."

"Sure." His reply was too fast and very eager. Dana smiled and she felt warmth creeping into her chest. It was a silly sort of schoolgirl reaction and even though she admonished herself for it, it was kind of a nice sensation.

"Great!" Now she was the one putting too much emphasis into things. Her voice was bubbling over like freshly popped champagne. "See you soon then. Thanks Timon!"

"No problem... Dana."

The way he lingered over her name made her think of his lips and the tip of his tongue. Even worse, once her mind took hold of the image, she couldn't let it go.

Dana headed back to the camper, chatting with Skylar to distract herself from her own excitement. She really did want to help Skylar find a mate and she certainly hadn't come with her on this trip hoping to find one of her own.

When Timon's truck pulled up, Skylar's eyes swiveled straight to her friend's face.

"Hey, Timon's back," she said, fake-casually.

"Yeah, I called him."

The cheeky, secretive smile Skylar made was almost as bad as pointing a finger and singing a childish song about who liked who in grade school.

"Don't look at me like that. I called him to help you," Dana said.

"Sure you did." Skylar drew out the 'sure' so the sarcasm level was extreme. She grinned and grabbed her purse, then trotted towards the truck. Dana followed bashfully, quickly looking away again when Timon's eyes met hers.

"So, where should I start?" Skylar leaned over, gripping the seats from her position in the back. To Dana, it seemed that Skylar had deliberately sat in the back to make sure she sat next to Timon.

"Start what?" Timon was focusing on the gentle curves of the road more than Skylar's dilemma.

"Yeah, start. Looking for a mate I mean. The bar? That's usually the place, don't you think?"

"No." His voice wasn't just firm, it held an element of horror. "Don't go to Last Chans Saloon. It's not a friendly place."

Skylar sat back, frowning.

"There's Brock's place." Timon glanced back as if to gauge her reaction. "Only if you're set on drinking."

"No, not really. I just thought, you know. Bars are where single people go. What's so bad about the Saloon?"

"It's full of rough types, okay? Just take my word for it," Timon said.

As usual, Skylar was incapable of understanding good advice. She fell silent, no doubt contemplating Timon's words and deciding what 'rough' meant to Timon, and if it meant the same thing to her. As they pulled up by the café, she jumped down out of the truck, waving as she hurried off.

"I just have something important to do." She winked hammily at Dana. "See you later."

Dana watched her go, very aware that she was now alone with Timon.

"I was surprised that you called." His tone was friendly, but the delivery was awkward.

God help her, but she found it cute.

"I actually wanted to talk to you about Skylar," Dana said, desperate to take control of the situation—to deflect anything personal that might be building between them. "I know we asked before, but do you really know anyone here who might hook up with her?"

He shook his head. "I really don't. Florence is the way to go."

"She told us no." Dana chose to leave out the part about her own match. "It was pretty harsh. She told Skylar there was no mate here for her. It really upset her. Skylar's a bit crazy sometimes—okay, a lot crazy—but she's got a good heart. She's been through a lot."

Timon nodded. "I think I can see that. But without Florence, I really don't know what we can do. I'm happy to meet up later and talk about it though, if you want."

Dana broke into a smile. Timon's answering expression was just as genuine. Intensity seemed to grow between them as their eyes met. They both blinked, trying to hide from it, but neither one could look away. Timon leaned forward, just slightly. It was enough to break the spell and Dana looked away, quickly getting out of the truck. Timon slammed his door shut on the other side and gave her an awkward wave as he hurried away up Main Street.

Dana spotted the café nearby and decided to head over for a coffee. Maybe she could talk to Florence about Skylar, or meet someone who could help her fix her up. But just as she crossed the street, a strange man collided with her.

"I'm so sorry." She held her hand up. "I didn't see you there."

He stopped, smiling at her. Even though he seemed

friendly, something was odd about his eyes. They were cold. No, not just cold. Gleaming, focused and almost feral.

The hairs on Dana's forearms stood up. It was a warm, sunny afternoon, but something about this guy made her feel like she was shivering in a dark alley at midnight.

"No problem." His voice was as smooth as his smile and just as false. "I wasn't looking where I was going. Hey, I saw you talking to Timon over there. It was Timon, wasn't it?"

"Yeah." Dana frowned, wondering why he was asking. "I'm not from around here, I'm sure you'd know better than me."

"Oh, I know Timon." He gave her a sharp, toothy smile. "I was just wondering how you knew him."

"I don't." Starting to feel scared, Dana turned to walk away. When she looked back over her shoulder, he waved. It did nothing to comfort her nerves.

"See you around!" he called. His voice was light, but he didn't sound happy. Why did he want information about Timon? Something about him was very off, and she hoped she didn't run into him again.

She hurried into the café, relieved to be somewhere safe. To her surprise, Skylar was at the counter, shuffling up a bunch of papers.

"Hey, what are you up to?" Dana was too tired by now to speculate.

"Oh, nothing." Skylar grinned, sticking the papers behind the counter.

"Where's Florence? I could do with a coffee."

"Oh, she's upstairs." Skylar waved vaguely at the spiral staircase at the rear of the room.

"What's she doing up there?"

"Finding a book or something." Skylar shrugged.

When Florence hadn't returned five minutes later, Dana

peered over the counter and examined the coffee machine. She's spent a couple of months working as a barista when she was at college. She thought she could just about make herself a latte if she needed to.

She went to the foot of the stairs. "Uh, Florence?" she called. "Just wondering if I could get a coffee down here? I can make it myself if you're tied up."

"What's that, dear?" came Florence's voice from far away.

Dana repeated her question with no more success.

Sighing, she took hold of the hand rail and stepped onto the vertiginous staircase.

When she reached the top, she couldn't have been more surprised at the sight that greeted her. It was a large, well-stocked library. Florence was on the far side of the room, stacking books.

Forgetting her bad mood and need for caffeine, Dana went over to join her.

Florence greeted her warmly and immediately began telling her about the books, and the value of running a library in Ragtown. She explained how she ran a small school for all the local kids, right there on a bunch of beanbags.

Dana got caught up in her passion and she lost track of time, until Skylar called to her from the bottom of the stairs, asking if they could go home soon.

Florence rolled her eyes sympathetically, and Dana went downstairs again.

"Listen, I really want to freshen up before I head into the bar. Do you think we could go home for a bit?" Skylar wheedled.

Dana goggled. "You want to go back home *now*? We haven't been here long."

"I forgot something I really need. Come on, it won't take

us that long to walk back, and we can always get a lift back in. If we bug Timon to take us up now, he won't want to come and get us later."

God, save me from Skylar logic.

"Okay. Let's do it." Dana sighed like she was getting forced into the first charge in a warzone.

They headed out of the café and found the road that led to the mine. The mountain trail was a little taxing, considering how little sleep she'd gotten the previous night, but Dana admitted that it was pretty.

"See?" Skylar grinned at her. "It's totally cool. We'll just take it slow."

They wandered up the track, Dana occasionally stopping to take a photo of a flower or bird. She was starting to enjoy the quiet of the trees and the fresh air. Maybe, this place isn't so bad, she thought.

Boom!

An almighty noise split the silence. Birds shrieked and burst into the sky. Dana froze, heart pounding. It sounded like an explosion, and it seemed to have come from farther ahead, in the same direction as their campsite. She stood still, too scared to run towards the sound but not knowing where else to go. As she looked around wildly, Skylar clung to her, whimpering.

In a panic, Dana pulled out her phone and pressed the first name that came up.

Timon.

He answered immediately and she tried to blurt out what had happened, aware that she wasn't making any sense. Skylar wasn't helping, yelling crazy theories.

"I'm sorry, Timon," Dana said. "I really didn't know who else to call."

"I'm on my way," was his only response.

His voice was calm, reassuring, and her heartbeat slowed a little. She was still scared, but she'd never had anyone come to her rescue like that before. It comforted her that he cared enough to drop everything to make sure she was okay.

CHAPTER 4

Timon

As Timon rushed out to his truck, he called Jagger.
Idiot. Idiot. Idiot.

He couldn't believe he'd recommended the mine to the girls as a safe place, only to have disaster strike when they'd barely been there a couple of hours.

Jagger answered just as Timon got his truck started.

"Hey, Timon. What's up?"

"Somethings going on at the mine."

"Shit, where the girls are?"

"Yeah. They just called me."

"What's happening?"

"I don't know, I'm on my way. I think it was an explosion."

"I'll be right there." Jagger rang off.

Timon wrenched the big truck onto the road, gunning

28

the engine. He had to get there, fast. His bear was roaring inside him at the thought of something happening to the girls.

I can't believe I sent them there!

He cursed himself over and over. He was supposed to be making sure they left town. That was the smart thing to do. If he had shut them down and told them to go, they wouldn't be in danger now.

His bear bristled beneath his skin. He could feel the power of the change running through his body like lightning, his thoughts becoming simplified as his animal threatened to take control of him.

I did this.

Blaming himself wouldn't help them now. The important thing was getting there and making sure they were okay.

It only took a few minutes to force his rusty old truck up the hill to the goldmine. He had his eyes peeled as he came up the old road, and relief flooded him as he saw Skylar and Dana huddled on a large rock around the corner from the mine.

"Are you guys okay?" He leapt out of the truck, reaching out to Dana. She let him take her hand, and he was startled at how tiny it was in his huge paw.

"We're okay." She blinked rapidly. "We were too scared to go up there."

"Come on." Timon gestured to his truck just as another huge vehicle came roaring up the road.

"There's Jagger." He waved at his friend as he passed, ushering the girls into his car. "Come on, let's go see if everything's okay."

The girls sat together on the front seat, holding hands. He could see they were both scared, but something about Dana was stoical. There was a depth to her that sung to him. It was like beneath her vulnerable exterior there was an underground lake, cool, still and completely undisturbed.

He wondered what it would take to reach that part of her —to taste it, even.

She glanced his way and he quickly turned his eyes back to the road. He had learned a long time ago not to try and comfort himself with little fantasies like that. They always ended in pain.

Jagger pulled up next to the RV and Timon parked beside him. They both looked up at the mine, observing the plume of dust rising into the air not far from the main entrance.

"Looks like a fall in. Was anyone in there?" Jagger asked, looking around.

"I don't think so. It's been abandoned for a long while now. Did you girls see anyone up there?" Timon asked.

Both Dana and Skylar shook their heads. They'd climbed out of the truck, but were standing close by, ready to leap back inside.

A great shadow suddenly blocked out the sun. Dana cowered and Skylar covered her head, but Timon and Jagger looked up, blinking as the light glowed around a huge set of leathery wings.

"Sorry," a deep voice bellowed. The dragon's voice was rough and barely human, and thick black smoke poured through his nostrils. "Didn't mean to scare you all!"

"What in the damn hell—?" Jagger cursed at the sky. "You mad bastards!"

Timon scowled. "Who is that? It's not Callan."

"No, but they're all fucking filthy pyros." Jagger rolled his eyes. "What are you doing up there?" he demanded of the dragon.

"Hide and seek, boss! Had a bit of fire go outside the expected range. No biggie!"

Jagger cursed and started stalking up the dirt track.

"You take care of the girls. I've got to go and talk to these fools. They should know better."

"Sure," Timon answered.

Jagger muttered to himself as he walked away, shaking his head.

Timon turned around, seeing confusion in the girls' faces. "Dragons," he said with an exaggerated eye roll.

Dana flashed a small smile. *Good.* They didn't seem scared anymore.

"Let's take a look at your RV." As he walked past them to check it out, he noticed that the big vehicle was listing to one side. When he got close, his worst fears were confirmed.

"Two tires are blown, and your backup tire as well."

"Is that bad?" Skylar asked innocently.

Timon laughed, shaking his head. "Yeah. It's pretty bad. Your RV won't be going anywhere for a while."

"But we'll be stuck out here!" Dana cried. "What are we going to do?"

Timon stood up, rubbing his chin. "We'll have to get it fixed. But you can't live in it like this. And I don't want you girls staying up here by yourselves," he said slowly. "I guess I could tow it back into town and you could park it in my backyard?"

"Does your sister live with you?" Dana asked.

Timon chuckled. "Yes. She does. But she won't mind." He looked up at the sky, shaking his head. "I used to live alone, now suddenly I'm living with three women."

Dana laughed.

He backed up his truck and started the heavy work of hooking the RV to it. "It'll take a few days at least to get the tires in. So, I hope it's comfortable enough at my place for you guys."

"I'm sure we'll manage." Skylar waved a hand dismissively, and climbed back into the car.

"Need any help?" Dana asked.

"No, I'm good," he replied, but she stayed to watch him work, and he felt a warm flush on his neck at the unexpected attention.

They climbed into the cab together, Skylar still talking about going to the bar and Timon trying to talk her out of it. He was trying to tell her about Brock's homemade beer when they pulled up into the driveway, with Skylar saying she didn't drink moonshine.

"It's not moonshine! It's artisan beer! I'm telling you, ask Rayleigh—"

"Save it, Timon," Dana muttered as she got out of the truck. "Once she's made up her mind, there's no changing it."

"It's just that this is dangerous. Skylar can't just go wandering into the Saloon," he protested.

"Even better. Skylar tends to find danger before it can find her," Dana replied ruefully, rolling her eyes.

Timon had a large front yard with a wide driveway down one side that led to an overgrown backyard. Since no one felt like cutting through a literal jungle of waist high weeds, they decided to drop the RV by the side fence.

Just as they'd folded out the canopy and started pulling out folding chairs, Florence came walking up the street. She waved enthusiastically, grinning from ear to ear.

Skylar barreled towards her, jumping up and down like an excitable puppy. "You did it, didn't you! You found my match!"

"No." Florence sidestepped, giving Skylar an annoyed glance. "That's not why I'm here."

"But, why—"

Skylar trotted after Florence as she made her way up the drive, in Timon's direction.

She's not here to talk to me, is she? he wondered. Then he looked over at Dana and felt angry with himself that he was daring to hope. He didn't want a mate. He couldn't have one. Florence was crazy and probably just there to sell him coffee beans or something.

"Timon, Dana, I have fantastic news for you."

His stomach dropped. She had *that look*. That self-satisfied, know-it-all look that he had seen enough times by now.

"No." He didn't say it with emotion, just a flat-out denial. "No." Maybe if he said it enough, she would just go away.

"Too bad, Timon, the numbers don't lie." Florence grinned and flung her arms wide. "You're a match! Dana, you and Timon are one of the strongest matches I've ever seen in this town!"

Dana gaped. "No," she murmured, as an array of emotions passed across her face.

Skylar put her hands on her hips, mouth hanging open in shock. She clearly had a lot to say but couldn't decide where to start. Dana was just shaking her head, still saying 'no' as if that single word could force Florence to back off and say she made a mistake.

But Timon had seen Florence work before. He knew how this worked. Maybe, if he could have stopped her before she made the announcement... But he hadn't. He had let her speak and now the words were out there, binding him to Dana, like it or not.

The conversations of the women drifted into background noise as his inner panic overtook him.

This couldn't be.

It was his worst fear and his greatest dream, both coming true at the same time.

CHAPTER 5

Dana

Dana took a quick step back. Shock poured through her, ice cold and searing flame at once. Goosebumps and sweat prickled all over her body.

Matched with a shifter. This was turning into one of the worst days of her life. She suddenly wanted to put as much distance between Florence and Timon as possible. Timon had taken a step away as well and the poor guy was somewhere between ashen and sickly pale. His strange, different-colored eyes flickered over Florence. Clearly he was as shocked as she was.

"What the hell is going on here?" Dana rounded on Florence, barely keeping her voice in check. "You can't just walk up to me and tell me I have a match. I didn't ask for one, and I don't want one."

Dismay flashed across Florence's face, but it was rapidly

covered with a bright smile. "Don't be silly, my dear. It's great news! My matches never fail."

"Well, this one is going to." Dana took a step closer. "You can't just match me up without even asking. It's a breach of privacy. I mean, it's probably illegal."

Florence's eyebrows drew together. "But I did receive an application. I have it right here."

"That's not possible!" Dana's shock made her voice high and strained.

"Ah..." Skylar raised her hand in an embarrassed little wave. "I might have something to admit, here."

Dana turned on her friend. "What did you do?"

"I-I filled out an application. I put it in before. I didn't expect—"

"Skylar! Why the hell would you do something like that?" Dana hissed, fists clenched at her sides.

Skylar's eyes were big and earnest. "I know you're lonely, no matter how much you deny it. And I just wanted to see what sorts of answers would get you matched."

It was Florence's turn to take a step forward, index finger jabbing at Skylar's face. "You cannot use my service as an experiment," she snapped. "Dana's right. This is a breach of privacy and I'm sorry for my part in it."

Skylar wrapped her arms around herself and shook her head.

"I know I shouldn't have dragged Dana here without telling her where we were going. Putting in the application for her was low. I get that and I feel bad, okay? But it's not fair that she got matched and I didn't. What was so special about her application, anyway?"

She looked at Florence beseechingly, but the curvy squirrel shifter merely glared at her through her silly red glasses.

"Can you check again? Maybe you made a mistake," Skylar tried again, lip trembling.

"There was no mistake," Florence snapped, hands on hips. "Dana's application was honest and yours wasn't. That's all I have to say on the matter. You should give this up, Skylar. There's no match for you here."

Florence turned her back on Skylar's disappointed face and flounced away. The three of them shot awkward glances at each other. Dana was trying hard not to notice how hot Timon was. She'd been kind of admiring his quirky good looks before Florence's proclamation, but now it was as if they had really come alive to her.

And apparently, we are meant to be...

She shook her head.

No. Not happening.

Looking at Timon only made the situation worse. Swiftly, her feelings polarized to anger and she aimed it at the person responsible.

"How dare you!" she yelled at Skylar. She had saved up too much frustration over the course of the day and now it was coming out as fury. "First you bring me here, park the RV in the middle of town, get us attacked by wild animals, drag me all over the fucking place, then you use my details on a match-making application?"

Skylar was still all puffed up with self-righteous indignation. "You got a match. What have you got to complain about?" she spat.

"I didn't want a match!"

"I've got to go," Timon announced abruptly. Before Dana could say anything, he turned and shambled off, shoulders hunched as if he needed to protect himself.

She felt bad that they'd scared him off. He offered to let them stay before he knew about the whole match business—

he was probably regretting it now. And, to her surprise, that thought kind of hurt. She couldn't help worrying about Timon's feelings and if it would affect his view of her.

Do I like the guy? Really?

As Dana opened her mouth to yell at Skylar again, Piper came trotting up the road. She had a huge cake box balanced on her arms and four coffees dancing precariously on top of it.

"Coffee break, girls?" she called. Dana hurried to help her, and Piper handed out the drinks while she grabbed some chairs and arranged them on the lawn, around an upturned crate that she guessed could serve as a table.

"I got us all super creamy mochas. It's a new thing Florence is trying. I hope you like it," Piper said. She opened up the cake box to reveal a massive chocolate cake with swirls of perfect butter cream icing. "Triple layer chocolate cream mud cake," she announced. "One of Savannah's finest creations. She's the baker for the café."

Skylar sighed in delight as if it was something you could marry.

"Thanks, Piper. But what have we done to deserve this?" Dana asked, trying not to eye the delicious-looking cake too eagerly.

Skylar had no such reservations. She reached out, grabbed a slice and bit into it, not caring about the crumbs spilling into her lap.

Piper shrugged. "Call it a house-warming gift," she said, grinning. She took a slice, too, and plopped herself down in a chair with a contented sigh.

"It's so good," Skylar mumbled, mouth full of cake.

"Heaven," Dana agreed. There was something deeply satisfying about eating gooey cake with your hands.

When Piper was done, she licked her fingers efficiently

and straightened up, her golden-brown eyes turning serious. "So, you guys want to tell me what's going on here? I saw Florence storming down the street like a thundercloud. Then Timon passed by looking like he was getting chased by wasps. And *then* I get home and you guys are having a Mexican standoff on the lawn."

Dana sighed and shot a glance at Skylar who was gazing off into the distance, as if it had nothing to do with her. "Only my best friend screwing me left right and center," she muttered.

Skylar groaned. "I *said* I was sorry! I just want to get matched so bad. I thought if I put your application in it would help me with mine. I never expected you to get matched at all—especially with Timon."

Piper's eyebrows shot up over the edge of her coffee cup. She swallowed too fast and shook her head, eyes watering. "Whoa, wait. Hold up... Timon? You were matched with Timon?"

"Yeah." Dana picked at her cake. "Florence said it's a strong one, too."

As she spoke the words, she wondered what the difference was between a strong match and a weak one. From what she had learned already, all the matches were strong. Fated and unbreakable. Did she even have any say in it?

"That's great news!" Piper exclaimed.

"It's not great news. Timon and I are not right for each other," Dana almost shouted. "And now he's gotten the wrong idea, and it's all Skylar's fault!" she finished, scowling at her friend.

"Dana, please forgive me." Skylar's eyes were full of tears. "I wasn't thinking straight. I'm really sorry and I'll apologize to Timon too. I had no right to get into your private life like that. I don't want to lose you over this."

Dana sighed, knowing that she still loved Skylar. She would never abandon her.

"I'm just mad, Sky," she said softly. "I will always be your friend, but you really betrayed me today. I can't just trust you again straight away."

"I understand." Skylar nodded, looking hopeful. "I promise, I won't meddle anymore, and I'll always tell you the truth."

Dana looked at her evenly. "Okay." She wasn't cool. Not yet. And it would be a while before she was.

Piper leaned over, nudging Dana's arm.

"So, matched with Timon, huh? Any thoughts?"

Dana's first reaction was to say something sarcastic, but those strange eyes rose in her memory. Beautiful eyes. Eyes holding something deep inside where he had never let another soul in. She had to admit, part of her was fascinated by the big, gruff bear. That didn't mean a thing though. She wasn't looking for a relationship and she certainly wasn't looking for a shifter. Florence screwed up and that's all there was to it.

Dana shook her head absently at Piper. She really did not have any thoughts. More rightly, those she did have were far too complicated to put into words.

CHAPTER 6

Timon

The shop had been busy most of the night and Timon felt proud of his little pizza place. Something that had been a half-baked idea was really working out —not just for him, but for the town.

The combination of Florence's coffee, Savannah's cakes and his pizza was creating a little community hub in the center of Ragtown. Rowan's little garden was also adding a spot of color in the otherwise dry lots, and plenty of shifters who previously had rarely seen the light of day were now regulars at these places.

Now all the customers had cleared out and Timon was cleaning up, wiping benches and sweeping the floor. He enjoyed every simple task, taking real pride in his work and the fact that not only did he have a business, but he ran it very well.

It was pretty amazing to him that he could do anything well at all, after the life he'd had.

But, after wiping down the counter for the sixth time, he had to admit that tonight had nothing to do with professional pride. He was worried about going home.

As he'd told Dana, he'd been living alone his entire life, and now he had three women around him. Getting used to his sister had been hard enough, but at least they were alike in a lot of ways. On the other hand, Skylar was like a flag, snapping in the breeze... Noisy, erratic and unpredictable. And Dana... Well.

Dana was supposed to be his mate.

For a moment, he allowed himself to think about her—about those green eyes, as bright and clear as a woodland forest. About the cute scattering of freckles across her nose. About the careless way her hair flicked up at the ends. She was like something from a fairytale—a pixie or a forest sprite—

Of course, she looks like a fairy tale to me, he thought, clenching his fists to dismiss the thought. *But I'm a fucking nightmare to her.*

It didn't matter if they were matched. He was not going to get involved with anyone, especially someone as lovely as Dana. No matter how much his bear growled and paced inside him, he would not be chasing after Dana to give her his mate mark.

She didn't even like him, anyway. She'd been horrified when Florence announced their match. Thinking about her was only leading him into painful places that he would rather not visit. Far better to focus on wiping down the bench. For the seventh time.

His bear gave a plaintive sigh, but he chose to ignore it.

If he wasn't so drawn to her, this situation would be so

much easier. It was nothing like that time when Florence had matched him with Kelly—Aidan's mate. He'd known from the beginning that she wasn't right for him. But Dana, with her calm, intelligent, caring nature, had gotten under his skin. His bear was insisting she was his mate. He knew it was wrong, but he had no clue how he was supposed to stop thinking about her.

He distracted himself by walking around the shop, pushing chairs in and tidying the tables. It was getting very late now, and he waved to Savannah as she passed by on her way out from the coffee shop.

After he was satisfied with the cleaning, he took the trash out the back. Just as he was throwing it in the dumpster, a low, warning growl cut through the night-time quiet.

Bear.

The hair on the back of his neck rose. He listened carefully. Was it a friend or enemy? He wasn't sure, and the sound didn't come again.

He didn't like it though. Conflict in Ragtown was a lot less common than it used to be, but enough bad things had happened over the years that he was always on the alert.

A split-second later, he took off at a run.

In the middle of Main Street was a huge brown bear, lumbering around, swiping at shadows. At its left flank was a little golden fox with comically large ears, nose to the ground, sniffing industriously. Timon skidded to a stop, kicking up a cloud of dust.

At the sound of his approach, they turned around.

"What's going on here?" he called. They both looked at him with surprise and hurried over.

Rowan shifted, picking up a shirt and pair of pants from the side of the road and dressing hurriedly. Meanwhile,

Nikita stayed in bear form, huffing through her nose as she searched for a scent.

"Someone's been prowling around the back of Florence's cafe. A stranger. Male," Rowan explained.

"Didn't you see him?"

"Not really. Just been trying to follow the scent, but the wind's chasing it away."

"More intruders," Timon muttered, peering down the dark street. "Wonder what he was doing here."

Rowan shrugged. "No idea."

Timon stroked his chin, thinking. "Well, I'll keep an eye out for him. Let Jagger know, too."

"Doing it now." Rowan held up her phone and gave him a mock salute.

He shook his head, grinning as he headed back to the pizza parlor. But as he entered the empty shop, there was a flare of sensation up his back, as his bear registered some kind of threat. It snarled and he looked around in confusion. He was one of the biggest bears around and it wasn't often that his bear felt challenged.

Of course, there was no one in the shop. There was nowhere for anyone to hide. He turned off the lights, telling his animal it was a false alarm.

Only once the room was fully dark did he notice the figure standing outside.

It was male, over six feet tall, and although he couldn't make out his features, he sensed that it wasn't someone he knew.

He went to the door, but the keys weren't in the lock—they were in the back door, and by the time he'd retrieved them and stepped outside, the figure had gone.

Timon inhaled hard, his gaze sweeping up and down the street—right, toward the road that led out of the town, and left, toward the forest. But there was no sign of the man, and barely any trace of his scent. Who disappears like that?

A little frustrated, he locked up and began to make his way home. Just one more screwy thing to add to a day of screwy things. He felt like he had spent the entire day jumping through hoops. He was looking forward to going to bed and hopefully, the girls would all be asleep.

BUT WHEN TIMON approached his house, he saw the kitchen light was still on. Someone was silhouetted against the window. A small, dark-haired someone.

His heart sank and lurched at the same time.

Dana.

Why did she fill him with such opposite feelings? It was confusing the hell out of him. And way more than a simple bear like him could cope with.

He was tempted to go right to bed without speaking to her. *But that would be weird*, his human side reminded him. Besides, he'd been looking forward to taking a chunk out of the hunk of deer meat that was currently filling up his fridge.

When he went through the house and into the kitchen, Dana was sitting at the table, huddled over a hot drink. He thought she looked even smaller than he remembered, and when she looked up her face was drawn, and her eyes were red with dark circles underneath them. There was a pain in his chest, right where his heart was, and suddenly all he wanted to do was rush across the room and hold her.

"What's wrong?" he said.

Her eyes had widened at the sight of him, and she looked guilty. "I hope you don't mind me being here?" she said in a strained voice.

"Course not." Wanting her to feel comfortable, he forced his lips into a smile. Smiling still didn't come naturally to him, and it was an effort for his facial muscles to form the expression. But when a ghost of a smile crept onto her face, he knew it had been the right thing to do.

Suddenly remembering that human females were often intimidated by his bulk, he pulled out a chair opposite her and sat down.

"I hope you don't mind me stealing your cocoa, either." Her eyes flickered toward his and away again, with that bright flash of green that lit him up inside.

"Take whatever you need. I want you to feel at home."

She looked up and fixed him with a serious look.

"That's not a great idea. I don't want to get comfortable here because I know I'm not going to stay."

His bear let out a growl at the idea of her trying to leave and he hid it with extreme effort.

"I see your point, I guess."

"I'm not here looking for a mate. I just want to help out my friend. I'm not comfortable around shifters. Do you understand?"

"Yeah. Of course." He didn't, but it was up to her to tell him if she wanted to. If she didn't like being around shifters, then Ragtown was not the greatest place for her. And he was not the right guy.

His bear hated the idea though, with every inch of its furry being. The longer they talked, the more it pushed its way to the surface. It had always been a wild beast, raw and unchained. He let it loose far too often. Now it was reacting to Dana and he was having trouble holding it in.

"So, it's just a terrible idea." Dana was saying. Timon was aware he had missed part of the conversation, but he couldn't do a thing about that. It was all he could do to keep his bear in check.

Claim her. Mate her. Possess her.

Yeah, this was going great.

As she fixed him with a serious stare, he made a supreme effort to force the bear down and smile at her. She kept talking about Skylar finding a match and Timon took a few deep breaths, finally suppressing his animal so he could focus on the conversation instead of her incredible scent.

"Timon, are you listening?" she demanded.

He shook himself mentally. "O-of course I am," he stuttered, caught in the headlight glare of those green eyes.

Eyes that now flashed with guilt as she shoved her chair back and stood up. "I'm sorry, I'm keeping you up."

Before he could say anything else, she was gone.

Damn.

His bear cried out in frustration, but he shushed it up. It was for the best. There were good reasons why he couldn't have a mate. He was not going to bind her to a person that literally had bad luck woven through his bones.

CHAPTER 7

Dana

*D*ana woke with some confusion. She barely remembered putting herself to bed at all, and now there was this incredible din just outside the window.

She staggered up, looking around. She remembered having cocoa with Timon, trying to explain how it just couldn't work between them. She had shuffled away soon after that because the longer she looked at him, the more intense her feelings became.

Being near him was exhilarating. She couldn't deny that. It didn't matter what her instincts told her though. Her mind needed to be in charge at all times. It was the only way to keep herself safe.

The clanging outside the window turned into a massive cacophony of sound, as if the cookware section of a department store was getting raided. She charged through the RV and flung open the door.

It was Skylar, of course. As usual, her actions were completely indefinable to the onlooker.

"What the hell are you doing?"

Skylar was under a table reaching for a large pot when Dana asked her question and she sat up suddenly, banging her head on the table.

"Ow! You scared me."

"And you woke me up! What the fuck are you doing?"

"I'm trying to make breakfast."

"You sound like you're trying to learn the drums. Emphasis on the word *try*."

"Well, the storage compartment fell open." Skylar crawled across the lawn, gathering pots and pans. "It's not my fault."

"Please, let's go and find some coffee." Dana yawned. "It's too early for this. I'm just thankful you didn't set yourself on fire."

Skylar scowled and pointed the frying pan at her, about to make a point. But Timon broke the moment by coming down the front stairs.

Dana became aware that she was only in tiny shorts and a tank top. She resisted the urge to put her arms around herself, knowing that the gesture would draw his attention. But as he got closer, her nipples chose that exact moment to feel a chill and stiffen into dark points under the thin white fabric.

Jesus fucking Christ.

She folded her arms across her chest.

Hopefully that's not too conspicuous.

She smiled as Timon got closer and a warmth flooded her chest, loosening her up. He really was cute, especially when he did that half-smile of his, which he was doing now.

"Would you guys like to come in for breakfast?" he asked, a little awkwardly.

Skylar dropped her handfuls of cookware with a cascade of clanging. "Yes please, and thank you," she said and tore past them, almost tripping on the steps.

Dana grinned. "Yes, I'd love to. Please tell me you have coffee."

"I do, but nothing fancy."

"That's totally fine. So long as it's strong."

He laughed. "I like mine pretty strong. Let's see how you cope."

She laughed as well, amazed by how at ease she felt. "Yeah, maybe put some hairs on my chest."

"There's nothing wrong with your chest."

Dana crossed her arms over her breasts again, cheeks flaming. When she looked up, Timon was blushing too, but this did nothing to relieve her own embarrassment. They entered the kitchen with a stilted silence that was immediately evaporated by the energy of the place.

Piper had at least four pans going with bacon, egg, pancakes and sausages frying. Toast was popping up every few seconds and the thick scent of coffee hung underneath the other delicious accompaniments.

Skylar was sitting at the end of the table already stuffing her face and complimenting the chef at the same time. The fact she was only seconds ahead of them showed how hungry she must have been. Piper was efficiently loading plates and putting them on the table so everyone could tuck in.

"Sit, sit." Piper pointed with a spatula. "I'll make you guys a plate."

She turned around again, furiously hurling perfectly cooked bacon and eggs with juicy sausages onto big stone plates. She set them down in front of Timon and Dana and went back for their coffee.

Dana could not remember the last time someone spoiled her like this. Piper was just naturally a giving person and Dana hadn't known too many of those in her life.

In between bites, Dana shot the odd glance at Timon. Sometimes when she looked up, he was looking at her. They would both blush and look away, making Dana more nervous than she wanted to admit. She didn't like the way her heart seemed to go out to him without her permission. She could see hurt there in his soul and something in her wanted to soothe it.

She shoved away the emotions and focused on the food. Everyone was enjoying it so much that no one talked until silverware started to scrape across bare plates, each of them trying to mop up every last bite.

"So, what's the plan today?" Piper asked brightly.

"I'm going in to see Florence again," Skylar announced. "If she doesn't want to talk to me, then I'll hang out in the shop and just introduce myself to people."

Dana laughed. "You don't think that's a bit conspicuous?"

Skylar frowned at her. "I think it's pretty clear by now what I'm looking for. No one will be surprised."

"There must be someone here for you." Piper looked off into the distance as she tore into another piece of toast. "I haven't been here that long, but surely there are shifters here waiting to be matched."

"There most likely are," Timon said as he finished his bacon. "But you really need Florence's help. She's the one that's set up so many people here. It's dangerous to go up to the wrong people in Ragtown."

Skylar looked down, chewing on her lower lip.

"Still, I might have a walk around."

Timon scowled, shaking his head. "It's not smart for humans to just wander around out here. You should know that by now. Just last night there was a guy that we didn't recognize prowling around."

"Prowler?" Skylar asked quietly.

"Yeah. A strange guy hanging out near the parlor. Rowan and Nikita were fairly worried."

Everyone took notice of this statement and Dana was glad to have something to focus on. This comfortable, casual scene around the breakfast table was making her feel more connected with Timon. Even though Skylar tended to flap about like a noisy bird, Timon handled her gently.

There was a loud knock at the door. Timon stood up and looked down the hallway.

"Come in, Jagger!" he bellowed.

"Hey Timon." Jagger's big form entered through the doorway and he sat down at the end of the table. "Hope you don't mind me barging in so early in the morning."

"No, no. It's cool. We were just finishing breakfast."

"Sorry I didn't make more." Piper said apologetically. "I could cook up something—"

"No." Jagger smiled at her. "I ate already, thank you." He looked around the room, concern flashing in his eyes, then he turned back to Timon.

"I heard about the prowler from the girls. Did you see anything last night?"

"There was a guy hanging out in front of the shop," Timon said. "By the time I got outside he was gone. Very little scent. Kinda weird."

"What did he look like?"

"I couldn't see a thing in the dark. Tall though. Slender. Kind of spiky hair."

Piper sat down, staring at Timon with wide eyes.

"Well, we're concerned about the details." Jagger went on. "We don't want this guy hanging around long enough to make trouble." He turned from Timon to look straight at Skylar, then at Dana.

"You guys aren't safe here in a shifter town," he said firmly. "You've been told over and over again. I want you out of here before something can happen to you."

"Fine by me," Dana muttered, and she shot a secret glance at Timon to see his reaction.

"Yeah, maybe it's for the best." Piper was gripping her coffee with white knuckles, face tense. Her good humor seemed to have disappeared in the face of this news. "It sounds pretty dangerous."

"We'll put out some more patrols. I'll get some of the other guys involved, just to watch out," Jagger asked.

"Does anyone know where to look?" Piper asked. She was trying to make it sound casual, but she was drawn and nervous, her cup almost shaking as she gripped it tightly.

"No," Jagger said. "He's only been seen a couple of times. We'll just start running some extra patrols around sundown and you guys let me know if you see anything else, okay?"

"Sure thing." Timon walked him to the door, glancing at Dana on the way out. She flicked her gaze away, putting her eyes down. She didn't want to see him with so much concern on his face. It weakened her resolve.

CHAPTER 8

Timon

Once Jagger and Aiden had taken off, the others organized themselves for the day. Timon was finding himself completely bewildered as the women chatted and moved around quickly, getting ready. He retreated outside and waited for them, glad to have a few moments of respite from the hotbed of intense feminine energy his house had become.

When they all started walking, still talking and laughing loudly, he couldn't stop himself from smiling.

Yeah. They are noisy and unpredictable, but I think I kind of like it.

He had been alone for so long he hadn't known the difference between solitude and loneliness. But now he was starting to get it.

When they arrived in town Skylar made straight for the

coffee shop and Piper backed away, saying cryptically that she had somewhere to be. It was very unlike her to be so cagey, but Timon was far too distracted by Dana to think much about it.

When he said he had to go and set things up in the shop, he expected her to follow Skylar. Instead she followed after him.

"What are you doing?" Timon asked, his voice sharp with surprise.

"I'm coming in to help." She smiled up at him and it was an easy smile, full of promise. The sort of promise he couldn't believe in.

"Why?" he said, feeling as if all the intelligent words had disappeared from his brain leaving him with only the basic ones.

Dana smiled again and it was like the sun breaking through dark clouds. He could see questions in her eyes but she wasn't letting them hold her back.

Does she really just want to spend time with me?

"It's all really boring," he said doubtfully. "You won't enjoy it. Just scraping the ovens and cleaning the benches, prepping ingredients. Why don't you just head off with Skylar?"

"She's doing a disappearing act." Dana gestured towards the coffee shop and sure enough, Skylar was going in the opposite direction. "I've been abandoned. Come on, I'll help you set up."

Timon didn't know how to protest, or if he even wanted to. He opened up the back door, letting Dana in. The first thing he did was switch on the radio. The only station Ragtown could pick up was not overly stimulating, but they did play a decent selection of songs and he liked music while he worked.

To his surprise, by the time he'd turned on the lights,

Dana was already hard at work. She had bundles of fresh herbs, meat, cheese and vegetables laid out on the counter and she was chopping and separating everything into small bowls.

"You really know what you're doing," he said approvingly, moving over to watch.

"Well, it's pretty intuitive, isn't it?" She heaped grated mozzarella into a bowl and covered it. "You're going to want this stuff all done so that it's easy to throw the pizzas together later. I'm also guessing you make up the dough now, set it to rise for a while so all you have to do is roll it out later."

He grinned, shaking his head. "It might seem intuitive to you, but it took me weeks to learn this. Every night was just flour and toppings everywhere, I was practically hurling things on bases."

Dana grinned as she mixed some basil and pepper into a tomato sauce. "Well, I'm sure they still tasted great."

"Nobody complained. Not to my face, anyway."

They both laughed, and suddenly they were looking at each other... and looking at each other.

Timon was the first to tear his gaze away, his heartbeat speeding up.

When he could bring himself to look at her again, she was swishing her hips and mouthing the words to a song, apparently unconcerned.

Damn. It was more than a simple bear could take.

He forced himself to focus on his task, but a minute later, he realized he needed to get some flour and yeast from out the back.

"Just passing," he said nonchalantly as he prepared to squeeze past her.

"Okay." She pressed herself against the counter and stayed still.

He tried to press himself against the far wall, but he'd underestimated how little space there was and his pelvis brushed the full curve of her ass. Immediately, his cock sprung to life. Praying he'd gotten past her before she felt it, he escaped to the safety of the stock room. But when he risked a glance back at her, he saw that her cheeks were flaming.

He was stuck somewhere between mortified and curious. Maybe she hadn't minded?

That was dangerous territory. If she liked him, there was no way he'd be able to resist her.

Then the only future was both of them getting hurt.

As the day wore on, they talked more easily. Questions about the food became discussions on music, moving on to movies and books. They had a lot in common, but plenty of differing opinions as well.

The music had them both jiggling a bit as they hurried to get the ingredients together. Timon was sure he was imagining it, but every time he looked up, her eyes were on him. She was looking at him just as much as he was looking at her. And then, somehow they were close again, both of them reaching for the salt shaker.

She tried to scooch backwards and he tried to step around her, but they were caught fast. Hardly knowing what he was doing, Timon bent his head, and somehow his lips were inches from hers.

Her expression turned serious and her lips pursed a little. His bear rose inside him, urging him to kiss her, to wrap his arms around her. The blood roared in his ears, and he leaned even closer.

The microwave oven pinged.

Dana coughed and slid past him. The moment passed.

He returned to his work with an awkward frenzy. "Good song, huh?" He tried for enthusiasm, but it fell flat.

"Yeah! Good to dance to." Dana's tone was entirely false, and she kept her gaze fixed in front of her.

Timon cursed himself, mortified at what he'd almost done. He had to be strong. She didn't know about him; she had no idea what she was getting into. He had to be responsible for them both and protect her.

By staying far away from her.

They both worked steadily for a few minutes, the music from the radio fading into the background. Timon glanced up occasionally but Dana was no longer looking up at him. The silence drew out long enough to become awkward, but Timon didn't know how to break it, even if he wanted to.

He hurried to the front of the shop, opened the door and wiped down tables. He felt by this point he would do anything to get out of that cramped space with Dana. Any longer wrapped in her delicious scent and he wouldn't be able to control himself.

Looking out the front window, he saw Skylar walking down the street from the direction of the bar.

Timon's bear growled. Part of it was frustration, but he cared about Skylar and genuinely wanted to protect her.

Dana gave a little yelp, and immediately he was ashamed of letting it come to the surface. "She's been at the saloon. I told her not to go there," he said, more roughly than he'd intended.

"And I told you, she just can't take good advice. She'll do what she wants to do and if you tell her 'no' she's more likely to just go and do it." Dana's voice was equally sharp.

"I don't care." He was close to snarling. "She's human and she should be more careful. She's acting like a silly girl."

Dana looked hurt and Timon realized he might have put his foot in it by speaking without thinking.

"Don't worry," she said curtly. "I'll talk to her and we'll get out of your hair as soon as we can."

Timon moved back behind the counter, realizing he had done something wrong but so new to the ways of women that he had no clue what it was. Before he could start to figure it out Dana went out the back to wash her hands and clean herself up.

"That's me done for the day," she announced. "Hope I was more of a help than a hindrance."

She left by the back door before he could say anything. His chest hurt, just a little and he wished he could take his words back. He watched her cross the short distance between the two shops and meet Skylar over at the café. They went inside with Florence and Savannah, Florence gesturing and getting animated as she no doubt faced off with Skylar again.

Once the pizzas started coming out of the oven, Timon felt a little better. He had worked hard at his craft and he could now say with certainty that every pizza was as good as it could be. Returning to the soothing, repetitive actions of kneading dough and mixing toppings took his mind far from the puzzle of Dana and he welcomed the distraction.

Kelly was one of the first to come in, sniffing appreciatively.

"Hey, Kelly! How's your business going?" From her first day in town Kelly had decided that everyone in Ragtown could use her organizational skills, and she'd been hiring herself out with mixed success.

She beamed at him, looking much more relaxed than when they'd first met. Initially thrust together as a potential match, they later found out Florence was actually trying to match her with Aiden. They could laugh about it now, but at the time Timon thought it might literally kill him to live with her.

"Great!" She sat down at the counter. "A lot of people here in Ragtown are hoarders so they have endless stuff to organize. I'm also working regularly with Nikita and Ryker. It's much easier for them to do deliveries if I organize stuff for them."

"That's really great." Timon gave her a warm smile, happy that things were working out for her. "Now, what can I get for you?"

"Two please, one pepperoni and one Napolitano. I'm meeting Aiden at the park for lunch."

"Nice. Have you guys got the house organized yet?" The glint in his eye made it clear that he was referring to the relentless passion she had for creating order in any situation.

She winked. "You know it."

He laughed. "You should see what Piper has done to my place. She's worse than me."

Timon turned to get her pizzas. Garrett came in a few seconds later. He was holding baby Ariel and the twins were bouncing ahead of him, Holt walking proudly beside Garrett and holding the baby bag.

"Settle down you two!" he grumbled at the twins. Timon could see that he was frustrated, wrangling all the kids at once, but he wasn't growling seriously. The man's eyes shone with love and appreciation for his children. They didn't all have to be his blood to be considered his own.

It made Timon ache, deep in his chest. He longed for that kind of connection. Seeing it up close was like a knife between the ribs.

"I apologize, Timon," Garrett said ruefully. "I'm taking over your establishment. Pump out as many pizzas as you can and fire them in our direction. Savannah is creating a new confection and I'm banished."

Timon exchanged a rueful grin with him and started slipping more pizzas in the oven as he handed Kelly's over to her.

"I should build a playground out the back," Timon mentioned absentmindedly.

Kelly lit up like a torch.

"Yes! With slides and swings and stuff! So, the kids can play and eat. Timon, you're a genius!"

"Well, I might start with some coloring books first."

Kelly laughed and left with her pizzas. People started coming in by twos and threes and Timon was working so fast he barely had time to think. When Piper walked in his heart leaped. She looked like salvation.

"Piper! Can you get back here please?"

She shrugged assent, bumping into Ryker as she came towards the counter. He was just sitting down at his table and turned around, scowling. When he saw her breeze past, he opened his mouth, closed it again and stared after her as if she had stolen the words right from his lips.

Piper was withdrawn and quiet, barely looking up at him.

"Are you okay?"

"Sure." She put her hair back and grabbed an apron, before moving out the back to slice more toppings. He looked after her for a few minutes, realizing that something was very wrong, but also sensing that she wasn't going to tell him what it was. His confusion in the ways of dealing with women only deepened. Did he push for more and maybe upset her, or leave her alone and perhaps leave her feeling abandoned?

Thankfully, orders came rushing in and took the decision away from him. He worked steadily, but his thoughts kept slipping back to Dana. Now that she had been here, he couldn't stop seeing her in his mind.

All he had to do was look at the counter or the surrounding tables and it was as if she was there. He didn't have to imagine it, she had left the imprint of herself on his memory. His lips tingled and his fingertips burned. She had been right here, almost in his hands.

Meanwhile, Piper's nervous glances were starting to freak him out a bit, almost as if she was expecting him to disappear.

"Piper, are you sure everything is okay?"

"Yeah. Fine."

The answer was so clipped that he could almost feel it cut.

"Where did you go today?"

"Nowhere." She swirled dough thoughtfully. Suddenly she looked up, narrowing her eyes.

"Hey. Do you remember anything about the prowler you saw?"

"I told Jagger everything I remember. You were there." Timon couldn't help getting a bit snappy himself. Her strange behavior was really bugging him. He couldn't understand why such a small thing was upsetting her so much. After all, seeing strange guys wandering through Ragtown was not an oddity and she knew that by now. And whoever the prowler was, Timon was sure he and Piper were more than capable of dealing with him.

Piper just nodded. He had never seen her not in a talkative mood. He paced back out to the counter, glad that it was busy, and he didn't have to think.

When he decided he had to ask her again, he looked up to see her taking off her apron and getting ready to go.

"You're going?"

"Yeah. Sorry."

She turned and left by the back door. Timon's uneasiness grew. Even though Piper had been here a few weeks, they had never discussed why she had come. She hadn't volunteered any information about their family.

He had stayed away from the subject because he was afraid to ask, but he assumed she'd tell him when she felt it was right. He also admitted to a heavy dose of dread that rose whenever he thought about his past. He was bad luck and that's all he could remember.

But now he had the sense that Piper was trailing something from the past, something that could be bad news for both of them.

CHAPTER 9

Dana

The sun was glinting dark gold across the buildings outside, throwing out long shadows. They had been in the café for a few hours and Dana's ears were ringing from the constant back and forth between Florence and Skylar. She needed to get out of the tense atmosphere and clear her head.

Dana sighed as she stepped out onto the street, feeling a cool breeze whipping up along the ground. The combination of warm sun and cool air on skin soothed her mind. She was too far out of her comfort zone. The last few days had been relentless and she desperately needed a break.

Her attraction to Timon was making the whole situation worse. It would be so much easier if she and Skylar could just drive out of town.

The café door opened behind her, then slammed shut. She sighed. Her moment of peace was over.

"I don't know what her problem is!" Skylar appeared in front of her, arms crossed angrily. "Ragtown is full of lonely shifters. Surely one of them would be interested in me!"

She practically posed against the light of the setting sun, flexing her body as if she was a model in front of the camera. In spite of her exhaustion, Dana had to giggle.

Skylar was beautiful, with her tall frame and violently colored hair. In the fading light the red and blonde streaks closely resembled the sunset and her tight jeans and blouse showed off her figure.

"I don't think you should take it as a personal insult, Sky." She shook her head. "Finding a mate is not the same thing as getting hit on in a bar."

"Easy for you to say. You have a mate." Skylar sounded a bit defensive as well as jealous.

"Apparently," Dana replied darkly, her low mood returning.

"I'm sure I have a mate. I know it." Skylar pouted. "I don't know why she's lying to me!"

"Skylar, maybe you should just chill out. It sounds like you've already chosen someone, and you just want miss matchmaker to confirm your choice."

Skylar gave her a crooked look. "What makes you think that?"

Dana shrugged. "You just seem pretty sure. As if you already found someone that you're interested in."

"Well, I don't."

"If you say so."

"But why won't Florence even talk to me?" Skylar moaned.

"Maybe due to a lack of honesty on your part?"

"Oh, I didn't lie," Skylar said in a wounded tone.

Dana burst out laughing. "Yes, you did! You lied on your application. You admitted it. Florence said she could never match you that way and that if you had to lie, you weren't the right candidate for Ragtown."

Skylar sighed and rolled her eyes, avoiding accountability without a word.

"Let's go get some pizza. I'm hungry." Dana grabbed her friend's hand and hurried towards the pizza parlor, hoping that Skylar wouldn't figure out that she was just eager to see Timon again.

When they sat down at the counter, Dana's eyes kept running over Timon's broad, muscular back. The second he turned around and their eyes met, she felt a bolt of electricity up her spine. He flashed a smile that he quickly covered, but it was obvious that the moment of connection had gone both ways.

"Hi, girls." Timon's tone was casual, even as he kept staring at Dana. "What do you want?"

"Extra cheese, extra pepperoni, extra mushrooms. Extra everything." Skylar's voice was pained and thick with false drama.

"Same for you?" Timon grinned.

"Yeah, sure," Dana said, knowing her own smile was too wide but she had no hope of toning it down.

While they were waiting for their pizza, Piper came in through the front door. She was looking over her shoulder, gathering her coat around herself. Her hair was messy and her face pale. She didn't crack a single smile or talk to anyone on the way in, which was very strange.

Timon stood in front of them, watching Piper with worried eyes.

"She does look down." Skylar paused halfway through a slice of pizza to look over her shoulder at Piper.

He shrugged. "She's been in and out of here all night looking like she's got death on her heels. I haven't got a clue what's bothering her. If you guys could have word with her, I'd appreciate it."

"Sure." Dana breathed the word out slowly, thrilled by how close Timon was to her. She allowed herself a brief fantasy of reaching up to kiss him before dropping her gaze and reminding herself she did not get involved with shifters.

Even if they are smoldering sexiness wrapped up in steel hard muscles.

Shit. Shut up.

Piper sat down beside them, her attention still drawn to the window. Her coat was still wrapped around her tightly, even though it was warm in the shop. When Timon put the pizza down in front of them, Dana and Skylar dug into the food, but Piper didn't even seem to notice it.

"Hey, guys!" Piper's voice was loud and strained. "Let's get out of here for a while! A road trip! Just take off. What do you say?"

Even Dana looked up at her in complete disbelief.

"We just got here!" Skylar protested.

"The RV is still broken," Dana answered.

"I'm not leaving the shop." Timon frowned, clearly more out of his depth than ever before.

Piper didn't bother to answer, looking down into her lap. The others waited for her to talk but she didn't, just kept staring and worrying at a loose thread on her cuff. Just as Dana couldn't take it anymore and had to speak, Piper stood up suddenly.

"I'll be back," she said. She nodded shortly before turning and walking out.

"Okay, what the fuck?" Skylar muttered.

"I know," Timon answered, wiping at his fingers with a towel and watching his sister disappear into the night. "It's been like that all night."

"Maybe she has a secret lover," Dana wondered aloud.

"I hope so," Timon said softly, thinking of all manner of trouble that a grumpy she-bear shifter could get into in Ragtown.

But within minutes, Piper was back. She walked right up to Dana and squeezed her shoulder.

"Look, I've got something to do, but don't walk home okay?" She handed Dana her keys. "Take my car. I've got to run."

She took off without saying goodbye, leaving the others dumbfounded.

"It's got to be a secret lover," Dana said lamely, trying to break the moment.

"Well, whatever it is, it's very weird." Skylar rolled her eyes and finished her soda with enough flippancy to imply she had never been weird in her life.

They finished their pizza quietly, Dana noticing that even though Timon focused on his work, he kept his eyes peeled for Piper.

She didn't come back.

The girls finished off their meal and headed out, waving to Timon. When they hit the curb Dana eyed Piper's keys uncertainly.

"She said to take the car." Skylar sounded hesitant.

"I know, but it's not far. Let's just walk."

Skylar shrugged as if it was all the same to her and they set off, Skylar clutching Dana's arm. At first, they joked about the day they'd had, but once they'd crossed the first street, the night felt oddly menacing.

It was too quiet. Cold was creeping through her clothes and the shadows leaned over them. There was no obvious reason to be afraid, but it was as if there were unfriendly eyes watching them from every angle. Dana started looking around nervously.

"What is it?" Skylar whispered.

"I don't know." Dana looked behind her and she was positive she saw a dark figure move behind a tree.

She was sure plenty of Ragtown residents shuffled around in the dark. The thing that made this so suspicious was the way it seemed to duck out of sight the second she turned around.

As if it was hiding from them.

"Skylar!" she hissed.

"What?"

"I saw something!"

"Let's move." Skylar started jogging, tugging Dana along with her. They kept up a steady pace until Skylar glanced back.

She let out a short scream. "I saw it too!"

She charged into a flat-out sprint. Dana tried to keep up with her and soon they were both running madly down the street, desperate to get to the safety of Timon's home.

When a black figure leapt out of the bushes and almost landed on them, both girls screamed loud enough to bust a dog's ears. They tried to run but the figure stopped in front of them, blocking their path. Just as Dana was about to melt into a puddle, the figure pulled off the hood of its jacket, revealing...Piper.

"What the hell?" Dana screamed. "You scared me half to death."

"I told you to take my car!" Piper yelled. The display of

aggression was so out of character that Dana backed up a step.

"We thought you might need it," she said in a timid voice. Piper shook her head.

"It doesn't matter now. Come on. I'll get you home."

Even though Piper was there and the dark shadow figure behind them could be passed off as a fear-induced hallucination, Dana didn't feel comforted at all.

As she followed Piper, her eyes darted in all directions, and she had the distinct sense they were being watched.

CHAPTER 10

Timon

Timon couldn't stop thinking about Dana. Sweet, beautiful Dana who seemed to like him, too. He knew it was dangerous to dream, that it would eventually get him hurt. But it made his bear purr and his veins fill with warmth.

And it was far more alluring than trying to understand Piper's sudden personality change. He wished he knew her well enough to ask what was going on. But he didn't trust that she wouldn't run, and he'd never see her again.

With everything locked up and the shop empty, Timon crossed the street, keeping his eyes open. All of Piper's strange behavior had started at the mention of strangers in Ragtown. But the street was almost deserted, and all the figures scurrying along—either on their way home or to the pub—were familiar.

When he got home, every light in the place was on. It looked like a damn lighthouse. That was weird. A thread of fear ran through him. Not for himself, but for Dana. Lovely Dana who was far too vulnerable in a place like Ragtown.

He picked up his pace and burst into the house.

The girls were sitting around the kitchen table. They all had a hot drink in front of them, but the bourbon was out too, and it looked like everyone had had a shot or two already.

They all looked at him with blank, frightened faces.

"What happened?" he demanded and his bear paced beneath his skin anxiously.

"Nothing, it's okay," Piper said hoarsely. She was clearly frightened and this enhanced the sliver of fear that had already infected him.

"I think someone was following us," Dana said quietly.

"What?" he said, and his bear growled, immediately pushing its way to the surface. It wanted to claw something to death. He just had to figure out who.

Timon looked around the table, taking in Piper's expression. He remembered her telling Dana to take the car, realizing that she would only have suggested it if she knew it was dangerous for them to walk home.

She knew something about what was going on.

He looked Dana and Skylar over and saw by their tired faces and drooping eyes they had little interest in their drinks. He needed them to go anyway, so he could start squeezing Piper for information.

"How about I walk you guys out to the RV," he said and he was surprised by how even his voice was. When Dana looked at him gratefully, he took her hand, helping her up. Skylar followed, rubbing her eyes.

"I won't let anything happen to you," he said as they crossed the porch. "You're safe here."

Dana nodded, looking back at him with something approaching trust. He wanted to enjoy the moment but the drive to protect her was so strong that he couldn't focus on his attraction to her. It was a whole bunch of new feelings for him and he was beginning to realize, you couldn't figure them out. All you could do was experience them.

Once he got the girls to the RV, he made sure they were safely locked inside before he turned back to the house. As he entered the kitchen those intense emotions were still hammering at him, and this time it was love and loyalty for his sister mixed in with fear and suspicion.

"Are you going to talk to me now?" His bear added a low growl to the words.

She nodded, taking a big gulp of bourbon.

"I know I said I didn't want to talk about anything before. But I was hoping it might all just go away. Now I know it won't. I have to tell you everything. You'll need a drink first." She pushed the bottle in his direction.

Timon sat down and poured himself a drink. He could tell, this shit was going to be heavy. He wasn't sure he was ready for it, but he was learning that the future was like that. It came whether you wanted it to or not.

Piper's breath trembled as she began, looking at her glass instead of him.

"Timon, you're the first son of an alpha. You should be in charge of our pack. It's rightfully yours. The thing is, they abandoned you as a baby because of your eyes. They expected you to die, but you were just left out in the cold. You were picked up by some local village woman."

"I don't remember any of that," Timon said carefully, "but I was told that I was an orphan and my first foster home had too many children to keep me. I ended up in the foster system, but no one could handle me. I couldn't handle my bear." He shrugged, looking out of the window at the darkness.

"I just let it consume me, my bear. I lived wild. It seemed to me the only way to live. Then one day I just kind of wandered into Ragtown, drawn by the scent of other shifters. I had trouble learning to be human. But I got there in the end."

"I understand." Her eyes shimmered gold. "It must have been torture to grow up as a shifter among humans. I was lucky, father favored me. Almost as much as he favored Vaughn."

"Vaughn?"

Piper kept her gaze steadily on his face. "Your brother. Next in line. Father is getting on and Vaughn knows he's next. The clan is falling apart, Timon. Innocent bears are getting hurt. Neither one is fit to rule. It's a disaster."

"How is that my problem?"

"Because they remember you. They know there was a first son. Parts of the clan have started to fight back, trying to overthrow father and Vaughn. He has told them that you'll come back. That settled them for a while, but the infighting will start again soon." She leaned forward, holding his gaze. "The whole clan will die, Timon."

He sighed, looking away again. He could feel that she genuinely cared about the people in the clan. It was hard for him to understand. They were the ones who abandoned him and left him alone.

"I have some sympathy for the situation," he said carefully. "But I can't do a better job. I'm not made to lead."

"You don't understand." Piper shook her head, tears

spilling down her cheeks. "They don't want you to come back—they want to kill you!"

"What?" he demanded. He was furious and baffled in equal measure.

"The only way father and Vaughn can stop the infighting and rule for good is to give the clan your head." She wiped at her cheeks, but tears kept coming. "They won't stop until you're dead, Timon. That's why I came here—to warn you, to help you."

Reality seemed to slide away from Timon as he considered her words. Not only did he have family out there, but they wanted to murder him. What a day this was.

He sighed. "So, what do we do? Is anyone on my side?"

"Terrified to move, most likely. Father wants their land and possessions, that's why he's ruling everyone by fear. That way he controls the resources. He's still there with his iron paw on their heads. It's Vaughn that's coming to kill you."

"That's why you've been weird. You're looking for him."

She nodded, face so tense from fear her eyes looked huge.

"Where is he?" Fury dropped from every word as his fist clenched.

"I don't know." She shook her head hopelessly. "He's here somewhere. I can feel him, smell him. I don't know where though—he's hiding from me."

Timon nodded slowly. He had never felt anything like this before. There was a sense of completion in it, knowing where he came from and why his life had been so lonely.

He needed closure, he realized. If they were coming to kill him, then so be it. His own family had wanted to kill him since the day he was born.

Let them come. He was ready.

CHAPTER 11

Dana

*W*aking up in the RV was starting to get old. Even though it was well set up and fairly comfortable, Dana was still missing the feel of a big, soft bed.

Maybe one with a nice hard piece of shifter in it.

Dana shook her head, trying to clear it of such naughty thoughts. What was the point of indulging? Nothing was going to happen between her and Timon. Far better to put it out of her mind.

I can't, said her mischievous side—the side of her that was governed by passion rather than sense.

Sighing, she gave Skylar a shove to wake her up, then put on a sweater and headed outside. Skylar followed closely as they went up the porch into the house.

As soon as they went into the kitchen, she got the coffee

started and sat down at the table, yawning and rubbing her face.

"Did you sleep okay?" Skylar asked.

"Yeah. Not bad."

"I didn't." She sat down across from Dana, scrubbing at her hair. "I feel like I've been running all night. The walk home was just too scary."

"I know, but I think we just freaked ourselves out over nothing," Dana said, doing her best to comfort her.

"Piper seemed pretty upset, though. I don't think it was *nothing*."

Dana frowned, focusing on her coffee. Maybe after breakfast she would be able to make some sense of her own thoughts.

"That's not all." Skylar sniffed, nearly crying. "You don't even want to bond with your match. It's just not fair. I'm not going to find anybody, and you get a shifter that you don't even want."

Dana groaned, expelling air from very deep in her chest. It was time to seek help with her problem.

"Well. I've been meaning to say something about that. I might, ah, kind of, like him."

Skylar stared at her for a few seconds, eyes going wide. Then she dumped the coffee on the table, spilling it spectacularly. She let out a whoop as she came around the table to hug her friend.

"That's great, Dana! Fantastic news."

Dana grinned, hugging her back. "Hey, calm down. I don't even know if he likes me back yet."

"Oh, no?" Skylar sat back down, sipping what was left of her coffee. "I think you do. If you don't, you're blind."

"Okay. There have been some signs of mutual affection." Dana looked away, bashfully.

"Listen to this girl." Skylar made a dismissive gesture. "You can't just say, 'he thinks I'm smokin' or something?'"

Dana giggled again, and it felt so good. Not just to let herself go and relax, but to lean on Skylar this way. They were best friends and in all the confusion, they seemed to have forgotten that.

Skylar made a sudden 'shh' gesture, looking up at the doorway. Timon and Piper came in, both of them looking drawn and tired. Dana looked over them with worry. Last night, it looked like Piper was coming down with something. Now it seemed like Timon had it too.

"Are you guys okay?" Dana tried to keep the alarm out of her voice.

"Yeah, fine." Timon sat at the table, but didn't get any coffee or food, just sat there staring at the tabletop and scratching his head.

Before Dana could ask him anything more, Piper moved quickly to the back door. The way they looked at each other suggested they'd picked up on something the girls couldn't make out with human senses. Before Dana could ask what it was, the two of them went outside again.

Skylar hurried to the window to see where they were going.

"What the fuck. They're shifting!" Skylar sounded shocked.

"This is too weird." Dana rushed over, too, raking her fingers through her hair. "I have no fucking clue what's happening here."

"You and me both."

She and Skylar kept looking out the window, watching as two huge brown bears disappeared into the distance.

After several long minutes, they emerged again, sniffing as they lumbered into the yard.

Skylar quickly sat down just before Piper and Timon came back in. Their clothes were rumpled from taking them off and putting them back on again. Piper had dried leaves twisted into her hair. Dana stayed standing, challenging them both for eye contact.

"What's going on?" Her voice was sharp.

"Yeah, come on. What's going on here?" Skylar's tone was kinder, but not by much.

Piper shook her head. Timon looked at Dana but couldn't hold her gaze.

"Not much. Just making sure there are no wild animals around."

Dana tried to engage them both further but only got short grunts in return. Timon wouldn't even look at her and she felt cold despair reaching from her guts into her throat.

Yesterday had been so wonderful. Making pizzas and chatting and singing along to the radio. Over the course of the whole day every expression and every word seemed to have been endowed with a deeper meaning. The looks they'd shared were like something palpable that Dana didn't just feel but carried away with her to treasure and touch.

And now, he couldn't even look at her.

If Timon really had no interest in her, maybe leaving was the best option. The trouble was, Skylar would never agree. Even though she kept bemoaning the fact that she didn't have a mate, Dana recognized the glint of secrecy in her eyes. The girl had a crush and it was plain to see, if you knew where to look. And worse, the truth was that Dana herself didn't even want to go anymore.

Piper and Timon finally grabbed some coffee, but neither of them bothered to get any food. The way they sat quietly staring into their cups reminded Dana of how people act right before a funeral.

"Can I make breakfast?" she said brightly, shocking the room. "You did such a good job the other day I thought maybe—"

"Not for me." Piper said in a low voice. "I'm really not hungry."

Dana turned her eyes to Timon, hoping for a word. Any word. When their eyes met, she saw him soften, the magic of his different colored eyes reaching out as if to take hold of her own. For a moment, she was sure that he would smile and say yes. Make her feel welcome and accepted just like yesterday.

Instead he looked away, shaking his head.

"No. Thank you, Dana."

The silence around the table seemed to reach fever pitch. Skylar looked around nervously and Piper quickly finished her coffee.

"I better get to the shop." Timon stood up suddenly.

"It's not even 8am yet!" Dana spluttered. "Why would you be—"

"No big deal. Sometimes I start early."

"Can I come and help?"

He looked down at her, face calm and impassive. "I don't need any help. Just stay here." He turned and walked out, far quicker than he needed to. Piper pointed in his direction and followed after him.

"What the fuck was all that about?" Dana said, her heart twisting in her chest.

This is what you get for caring. For daring to hope for love. For trusting shifters.

"I have no clue." Skylar put her cup on the sink. "But I gotta run, too."

"Where, for heaven's sake?"

"Just out. I won't be too long."

"If you're going to Florence again—"

Skylar laughed. "That's exactly where I'm going, of course!" She grinned and waved. "Just hang out here. Get some rest. You need it."

"Okay." Dana looked down into her cold coffee, feeling abandoned in every possible way. When Skylar left, she decided to find the bathroom and have a decent shower before figuring out what to do next. Life had suddenly become far too complicated.

Not that it had been simple before.

CHAPTER 12

Timon

After getting Piper settled in the shop, Timon got ready to leave again.

But she stood right in front of him, glaring as he tried to walk out. "Oh, no you don't," she said crossly.

"Piper." He rubbed her shoulder. "I'm just heading up to see Nikita and Ryker. I'll grab a few things and order a delivery for later in the week."

She narrowed her eyes at him. He smiled back.

She shook her index finger at him. "You'd better be back soon," she almost growled. "I'm trusting you."

He grinned. "I won't let you down."

The second he was through the back door he felt bad about his words. But there were things that he had to be alone to do. He was self-trained in solitude and having others around—even if they were caring for him—was such an alien feeling he knew he wouldn't be able to concentrate properly.

He was going to find Vaughn, he just needed to do it in his own way.

Heading straight for the forest, he shed his clothes as he came through the first line of trees. His bear roared free from his tight hold and he let it run, paws striking the ground as his lumbering bulk picked up speed. His heightened senses absorbed the forest, reminding him that he was a wild creature, not something that lived by the rules of society. He was an animal, more bear than human. He had spent so much time lately trying to fit in with Ragtown he had almost forgotten the freedom of living wild. Ignoring his hibernation this year had probably been a mistake. It always soothed the bond between bear and man.

But, if he had hibernated, he would never have met Dana.

He unleashed wild roars as he ran, feeling the forest tremble around him. Dana made him feel powerless and strong at the same time. He wished that he could focus purely on that feeling, and on winning her heart, without all that ridiculous clan crap ruining things.

He dropped his head and inhaled all the rich smells of the forest floor. Maybe if he could find his brother and sort this out, he could go back to making pizza and flirting with Dana. He knew the problems in his life couldn't be reduced to such simple terms, but he could hope.

As he passed through a meadow that ran by the river, he caught it—the scent that he was looking for. The only reason it stood out was because it was fresh.

And because it was almost identical to his own.

If it had been old, then he could have mistaken it for himself on one of his previous runs through the forest. Because it was new, he knew that it wasn't his own.

But so close, so very close.

Across the clearing, a branch snapped loudly. No forest creature was that clumsy. Someone was announcing their presence.

He turned and roared, as rage poured out of him in a primal torrent. Automatically, he stood up on his hind legs, taking in the details of the bear in front of him.

They were almost the same size, the other bear only a little smaller. Both were black bears with brown-tipped fur. The one main difference was the other's eyes—a soft glowing gold, just like Piper's.

Vaughn lifted on to his back legs, too, and roared. The sound was almost as mighty as Timon's. They both dropped down to all fours, swiping at the air with their paws and lowering their heads.

Timon tensed, bunching his huge shoulders.

Fuck this threat display shit. If he keeps it up, I'm just charging him.

But, to Timon's surprise, the bear suddenly shifted. Its massive form dwindled down, until a strange man stood before him, smaller, but big for a human. He smiled and stood still, holding his palms up in a gesture of peace.

"Hello, brother," he said softly.

Timon didn't trust him, not at all. Still, the guy was naked. He wasn't hiding any weapons. Timon took another deep sniff of the air, checking whether there was anyone else nearby. There was nothing.

Hesitantly, he forced his bear to retract and he shifted, too. For the first time, the brothers looked into each other's' eyes. Timon was shocked to find that just by looking, he knew this was his brother. The blood in their veins was identical.

"We don't need to fight, brother," Vaughn said softly.

"The fuck we don't! You came here to kill me!" Timon's pent up rage exploded in a roar.

Vaughn planted his hands on his hips with a dry, sarcastic laugh. "Oh, is that what she told you? Piper? Our sweet, scatter-brained sister. I'm sure you've known her long enough now to see how emotional she is. She just misheard. It's all a big misunderstanding."

"Right. Like you feeding me shit and calling it ice cream."

Vaughn laughed. "That's funny. Actually, we could use some humor around the clans. It's been pretty bad there."

"Because of you."

"No, no. I told you, it's all a big misunderstanding. Come home with me, and I'll show you."

"Even if I believed that Piper is so emotionally unstable that she could misunderstand something like this—which I don't, by the way—there's no way I'm going with you."

Not without fifty-seven fucking grenades and a shot gun, anyway.

Vaughn tilted his head to the side with a patient expression. "Brother, listen. We want you to come and lead us. All of us do. The whole clan wants to welcome you back to the fold. You can take your rightful place." He smiled, his eyes like chips of obsidian. "You can finally have a family."

Family. The word struck Timon in the chest like a truck. The one image that rose in his mind at the mention of the word 'family' was Dana.

He took a step back.

"You're full of shit, Vaughn."

"Oh? So why aren't you attacking me right now? Out of the goodness of your heart? Come on Timon, I know you. I know your blood. We have the same soul. If you really wanted to turn your back on the clan, you would have ripped my throat out the second I shifted." Vaughn gave another one of his freaky smiles and Timon bristled.

I might kill him just to stop him fucking smiling.

But Timon really didn't want to kill his brother. That would most likely mean killing his father, too. After only just finding out how much family he had, he didn't want his next action to be murdering them.

Still. Vaughn was a liar. It was obvious. He had purposes here that Timon could only guess at.

"You can stand here and make offers all day," Timon said tightly. "I don't want to lead the clan. I have enough trouble running a pizza shop. Go back to your own people."

"But that's perfect!" Vaughn smiled even more widely as if he knew it was freaking Timon out. "Come back with me, show yourself to the clan and tell them that you'll make me your heir. Then father and I can create order and you get to come back here."

"Create order?"

Vaughn opened his hands, expression regretful. "Sometimes a firm hand is needed. An alpha always has to think of the greater good. Sacrifices have to be made."

"I'm sure."

Vaughn kept talking, trying to convince Timon of the difficulties of leadership. Something definitely didn't smell right here.

Why was he bothering to talk, if all he needed was Timon's head?

Trying to catch him off guard, maybe. Trick him into coming along so they could murder him without his Ragtown family knowing.

Timon looked up, meeting his brothers' eyes. He didn't want to attack Vaughn and kill him. He didn't want to get a knife in the back, either.

85

"I'll have to think about this," he said.

"Of course." Vaughn nodded, sounding perfectly reasonable. "Take whatever time you need. I'll be waiting."

Timon gave his brother his back as he shifted and took off into the forest.

CHAPTER 13

Dana

Sitting on the steps of Timon's front porch, Dana sat and watched the day go by. She didn't feel like chasing after anyone. After everyone had left, she had found the solitude quite peaceful.

Hands gripped around a cup of tea, she watched the clouds on the skyline. Ragtown was a beautiful place, she had to admit. Even if some of the buildings and streets needed repair, the scenery of the small mountain settlement was breathtaking.

The time alone allowed Dana to think. The last few days had been a whirlwind of emotion that she'd happily let herself get swept up in. Skylar's enthusiasm and quest for love had at first distracted her, and then she'd been infected by it.

Timon was a shifter. When she'd watched him and Piper

shift this morning, she'd felt frightened of them both. She knew they weren't really a danger to her, but the fact that they were shifters had really hit home.

And she couldn't trust shifters.

They weren't people—they were fifty-percent animal. And they had to be selfish creatures—it was part of their survival instinct. The one that had taken her mother certainly hadn't cared that he was breaking up a happy home.

Dana's heart still sang every time she thought of Timon, but she cursed it for a traitor. She couldn't help the way she felt when she looked at him and that scared her.

A truck came rumbling up the street, distracting her from her dark thoughts. It was almost as big as the RV, and had a big crane hook on the back. It pulled to a stop in front of her and a tall guy jumped out and waved to her.

"Hey, I'm Lachlan, the mechanic."

"Oh, hi. Are you here to fix my RV?" She put her tea down and hurried over.

"Sure am." He grinned at her and his curly black hair fell untidily over his forehead as he pulled a massive jack out of the back of the truck.

"You're Dana?"

"Yeah."

"Everyone calls me Locky." He gave her another one of his huge smiles, then went over to the RV.

"Let's see what we can do for you. Damn! These things look melted on."

"Yeah my RV got into an argument with a dragon."

"Oh, boy." Locky laughed as he sat down to set up the jack. "I thought Callan had those guys all sorted out."

"They were playing, not fighting."

"Oh, that's what I meant. But dragon play is…Not exactly gentle."

"Are you a dragon, then?" Dana crossed her arms, immediately on the defensive. She'd gotten used to being around bears—well, Timon and Piper anyway—but dragons were a whole other level.

"No, no." He shook his head, examining the wheels.

She waited for him to go on, but he didn't. She wanted to ask what his connection was to Ragtown but maybe that was too personal. If he didn't want to share information, she shouldn't ask.

She went back to her spot on the porch, watching the sky, with the sound of Locky fixing the truck in the background.

After a while, he gave a sigh of satisfaction. "Okay, that's you all done. Are you heading into town?"

She hesitated for just a second, then nodded. Maybe she'd go to the café and speak to Florence—even though the meddling matchmaker was a shifter, too. Skylar had told her that Florence was a squirrel, but Dana was having trouble wrapping her head around that.

"Need a ride?"

She laughed. "No, thanks. Nothing here's more than a street away."

He laughed, too. "That's what I figured." He wiped his hands on his pants. "Nice town," he said, looking up and down the street.

"You know people here?"

He gave her a sideways glance. "Not really."

She could tell he didn't want to be asked about his connections. *Sheesh.* These shifters were a secretive bunch.

He jumped into the truck, taking off with a wave. She hurried over to Main Street, heading to the café. As she walked in, she spotted Florence and Savannah at a table by the counter, poring over a cookbook. They looked so cozy that her heart warmed at the sight.

Savannah jumped to her feet with a big smile. "Hi, what can I get you?"

"One of those creamy mochas would be great."

As Savannah moved over to the machine a series of thumps sounded overhead. Florence puffed her cheeks out.

"I'll just go check on the children, dear. April is up there but I think she's being a bad influence." Florence scuttled up the stairs as Savannah handed over the creamy, chocolatey monstrosity.

Dana sighed in pleasure as she took her first delicious sip. "Have you seen Skylar?" she asked.

Savannah frowned. "No. I haven't seen her all morning."

"Hmm…she was supposed to be here."

Behind them, the door jangled, and Skylar came in, her haze of red hair with blonde tips far more wild than usual. Her cheeks were flushed, and she was smiling mischievously.

Dana cocked an eyebrow at her. "Where have you been?"

"Nowhere. Just hanging out."

At that moment Florence came down the stairs as if drawn by Skylar's voice.

"You should be getting ready to leave." Florence advanced on them with her arms crossed against her curvy bust. "Dana needs to stay for Timon, but I told you, there's no mate for you here."

Skylar shrugged. "I'm not going anywhere, so you might as well make me a mocha."

For a second the two women glared at each other, then Florence turned around and stormed over to the coffee machine, clanging and smacking things around.

Savannah and Dana retreated to a safe distance, grinning.

"They'll get along. You'll see," Savannah whispered.

Dana smiled, thinking that she was probably right. Her amusement soon faded though as her troubles rose to the surface once more.

Savannah looked at her sideways, then darted behind the counter.

"Here." She put a slice of vanilla and strawberry cake on the table and gestured for Dana to sit down. "You look like you could use it."

Dana's eyes stung at the unexpected kindness. "Thank you." She picked up the spoon and took a bite. The sugar hit instantly calmed her and she pulled herself together again.

"You look sad, honey. Sad and confused." Savannah reached out to pat her arm.

"Yeah, that pretty much describes it."

"I know what it's like, I've been there."

Dana blinked. "You have?"

"Yeah. When I first came to town Garrett was sure he didn't want a mate. It was a painful, confusing time. But we got through it. We are just so in sync, you know. It's almost like I know what he's going to do before he does it." Her face lit up.

Dana nodded, sadness sitting heavily in her gut. She could feel the connection between her and Timon, but she didn't think it would ever be that strong.

And whatever he and Piper were up to at the moment— Dana didn't want any part of it. She was starting to get used to the town—to feel at home, even. But it seemed like there was so much danger, living just at arms' reach.

And on top of that, Timon was ignoring her. He didn't want a mate. Why should she stay here, putting herself in danger, if he didn't even want to give them a chance?

A flurry of giggles and thumping came from upstairs. Florence huffed loudly.

"I told you April was a bad influence! That baby dragon inside her is creating seven kinds of mischief!" she growled as she headed back up the stairs.

As Florence left, the front door chimed again and Rowan came in with a loud, cheerful greeting to everyone. Savannah jumped to her feet and went to make her coffee. It was obvious Savannah knew everyone and she knew what they liked.

"How's the garden doing?" Savannah called to her.

"Great!" Rowan sat down at the table opposite Dana. "I was worried that prowler was going to trash it, or steal my carrots or something, but so far it's all good."

Dana gripped her cup hard enough to put it in danger of shattering, and she wondered how Rowan seemed to not be bothered by the idea of a prowler.

Of course. She's a shifter, stupid. She can just shift right outta there. I can't.

Which was why a single, unmated girl like her didn't belong here—as Timon had warned her, the very first time they met.

Dana had lost her appetite. She tried to think about nicer things, but the only thoughts in her mind were dark and foreboding, no matter how hard she tried to shake them.

CHAPTER 14

Timon

*W*hen Timon arrived at the shop, Piper was already there, busily chopping tomatoes at the counter. She looked up and her customer-facing smile turned into a glare.

She threw her knife down and planted her hands on her hips. "I knew it! You didn't go to see Ryker at all."

"No. I knew I could find Vaughn if I went by myself." He tried to avoid her eyes.

"That's because he *wants* to find you! Timon, I'm serious. He wants to kill you. This is dangerous."

Timon shrugged as he went to the sink to wash his hands. "Everything in my life has been dangerous."

"This is different. It's a blood feud. They're not going to stop."

Timon sighed. "He says he doesn't want to kill me. That if I go home and give up control of the clan that's all he needs."

"He's lying. If you go back and say you're giving up your position, there will be a war."

"I have to try and choose the path of the least resistance." He kept his eyes on his hands, carefully washing the dirt out from under his nails.

"That is exactly how he will get you. He's counting on it. He and father think you're weak. If you don't go after them, it will prove them right. They will come and you have to be ready." She stepped closer, voice trembling.

He shook his head. "I'm ready for that. What am I if not a big, brawling beast?"

Piper looked at him crossly, hands still glued to her hips. She went to say something then thought better of it. Instead, she squeezed past him to get her coat.

"Give Vaughn my regards," he said moodily.

Her only response was to slam the door on her way out.

Timon went over to the counter to finish up the chopping and line up the bowls in the fridge. He didn't want to think about complicated clan politics. If he wanted to think about anything, it was Dana.

As if summoned by his thoughts, there was a knock at the door and her pretty face peeked in. She smiled when she saw him, and he felt his own expression automatically mirror hers. No matter how much trouble they were having, the reaction they had to each other just got stronger. He could feel it, like binding waves that joined her heart to his.

"Hey. I just thought I'd come in to talk." Her voice was soft, conciliatory.

"Sorry about this morning. Piper and I have some family stuff to deal with." He hurried back to the counter, eager to put some distance between them.

"Oh. I didn't think you had family. I mean, apart from Piper." She seemed genuinely surprised.

"Not really. Or, I wish I didn't."

"Oh." She looked down at her hands and he could sense her withdrawing. She had come in here to say something and now he was scaring her off, again.

He should say something, but words failed him, as usual. Instead, he turned to the oven, seeing whether it needed cleaning. It didn't. He was only torturing them both. She should get out of here. He didn't want her mixed up in any of this.

"So, are you and Skylar leaving soon?" He turned around again and caught her gaze, trying to keep his own expression neutral. She looked surprised and maybe even a little hurt.

Good. It was for the best in the long run.

"I suppose so. Skylar doesn't seem to be having any luck." She looked him right in the eyes and he saw that cute bottom lip tremble.

She inhaled and exhaled slowly. "Neither are we," she said in a rush, as if it was something she was determined to get out.

He looked away, pained. He couldn't keep doing this. His bear was fretting and grumbling inside him.

Claim her now, it urged him. *She's yours.*

He let out a low growl and Dana backed up a step. He shook his head, trying to clear his thoughts. The scent of her drew him to her like nothing else. He couldn't fight it.

"It's just impossible for me to have a mate." He grasped wildly for the right words, any words that could make her see that she should be with anyone other than himself. "All the stuff that's going on in my life—well. It's complicated."

"I see." Now she sounded detached, like she didn't care.

Good.

She pushed her sleeves up. "Well. I guess I'll help you make a couple of pizzas then. I don't have anything better to do."

"What about Skylar?"

"Around here somewhere. Probably arguing with Florence again."

Without waiting for a reply, she came back behind the counter and put on an apron. Then she reached for one of the mounds of dough he'd prepared and started to roll it out.

Okay. If she was cool about things, then he wasn't about to cause any more drama. He shrugged and reached for the flour.

They worked together for a while in silence.

Mind if I put the radio on?" Dana asked, her voice so loud in the quiet that he jumped. The truth was, he wasn't at all cool about things. Every nerve in his body was on edge, hyper-aware of her presence beside him.

"Not at all," he said gruffly, and the memory of them singing along to it the other day twinged in his chest.

He started on a few more pizza bases and when he reached past her for the sauce, he was too close to her. When she looked up at him, their faces were inches apart. He was enchanted all over again by her eyes. They were such a pale green, like sea pebbles or fresh new leaves. The little cap of black hair framed her pale face, bringing out her delicate features. Her lips made a little pink bow that he longed to kiss.

His blood was singing, his bear roaring. She half closed her eyes and pursed her lips and that was all it took.

He leaned down and suddenly their mouths met. Electricity zinged through his body and he almost jumped back, startled.

Almost.

Because the sensation of Dana's lips against his was about the most amazing thing in the whole world. Even better than he'd imagined—and he'd been imagining it a lot lately. She moved them back and forth a little, all soft and slippery, and then, to his amazement, the tip of her tongue darted out and licked his lower lip. He didn't get it at first, but then she put her small hands on his face and pulled him closer, and before he knew it, his own tongue was sliding into her sweet mouth, and she made a small sound. He pulled away, worried he'd done something wrong. But she grinned at him, her eyes and teeth all pretty and sparkly, and drew his mouth to hers again.

Dana looped her arms around his neck, and, acting on instinct, he lifted her right up and onto the counter. She wrapped her legs around him, putting her hands on his shoulders, and suddenly, their bodies were pressing together. His bear purred and it rose to the surface. The need in him was bone deep. He had never felt anything like this before, his entire body singing for her touch, thrilled by every trace of her fingers, every tiny movement of her lips.

Nervously at first, he let his hands roam up and down her back, feeling the outline of her bra beneath her shirt. He longed to touch her all over, for them both to be free of their clothes. Nothing else mattered, only the feel of her like satin in his hands, so soft and silky sweet, smelling like woman and a soft, gentle scent of woodland flowers.

When the door rattled, he stepped away from her. They turned their heads—it was just the wind. She laughed softly, her lips red from the pressure of his kisses, and reached for him again. But he backed farther away, hitting a nearby shelf and knocking into some pots and pans with a loud clang.

She frowned. "Timon?"

"You should go."

97

"Why?" Her smile dropped and she looked so hurt, it was all he could do not to go to her.

"Dana, it's complicated. I don't want you to get hurt and I shouldn't have lost control like that."

"But Timon—We—"

"There's too much you don't know. You should go, right now."

"Why don't you just tell me?"

"I can't," he said curtly, and turned to the oven, busying himself with rearranging the shelf.

Dana was silent for a few seconds, and he felt her eyes burning into his back. When he finally turned around, her eyes were unnaturally bright. His heart ached and more than anything, he wanted to take her in his arms again. But this was how it had to be. His life was dangerous, and it seemed to get worse every passing day. The best thing he could do for her was make sure she stayed far away from him. Maybe if he was firm enough and ended it now, he could save her from getting hurt later.

"Fine. Be like that," she said at last. She turned on her heel and slammed out of the shop.

CHAPTER 15

Dana

ana couldn't hold back her tears as she left the pizza parlor. They just kept flowing, and she felt like screaming.

She made her way around the side of the building, and wiped at her nose and cheeks, trying to pull herself together. Her chest constricted like her heart was trying to claw its way out. All morning she had been so torn, but after talking to Savannah, she had finally found the courage to go to Timon. To make herself vulnerable.

It was so hard for her to put herself out there. To trust anyone, especially a shifter, was huge. It was one of the hardest things she had ever done. But she'd told herself that love would find the way, that he wanted her as much as she wanted him, and everything would be okay if they just let go and allowed the feelings growing between them out to flourish.

What a ridiculous fool she'd been.

He wanted her. Big deal. Plenty of men had wanted her. But when it came to caring for her, supporting her, he was bailing out.

So what if his life was dangerous? None of that was supposed to matter to fated mates. Something beyond their control brought them together for exactly that reason—that they were there to help each other through their issues, because no one else could.

He obviously didn't see her that way.

She wandered across Main Street and went back to the cafe. She was lonely now as well as hurting and even though she wasn't ready to talk about it, she needed company.

Again, Skylar was not there.

"Where is she this time?" she asked Florence, who was cleaning the coffee machine.

"Skylar?" Florence replied without looking up. "Vanished again. She keeps saying she's going for a beer. I hope she's at Brock's and not the saloon. It's no place for a woman, even one like her."

Dana sniffed, feeling abandoned.

Florence finally looked up, and when she saw Dana's face, she gasped. "Gosh, what happened?" She rushed over to hug Dana.

"He rejected me. We got together, a bit. I thought things were going great. I understand this mate thing now. I really think I do. But then he backed off and made me leave." She bit down hard on her lower lip to stop herself from wailing.

Florence pulled back from the hug, gripping Dana's arms.

"That Timon is a ridiculous boy. I've known that since I

first came here. Stubborn as hell and withdrawn, like he's constantly in hibernation!" She rolled her eyes then leaned into Dana, smiling.

"That must be why he has such a strong mate."

"I'm not, I'm not strong. Look at me!"

"My dear. Crying like this is strength. It's Timon that's being weak, trying to fight this instead of embracing it. You are feeling the power of the bond while he wrestles with it." She sighed, lips tugging down in sympathy.

"You have to convince him, Dana. That's all there is to it. He is your mate and he will listen, you just need to break down that door."

Dana shook her head, sniffing, but Florence gave her a push. "At least get him to apologize. He should know better than to make a girl cry—any girl!"

"Thanks, Florence," Dana said and stepped outside. She wasn't going back into the pizza parlor. She wasn't convinced that she could talk him around and she was far too bruised right now to even try. She knew Florence was right. He would never come around on his own. He needed his walls broken down.

She just didn't think she was as strong as Florence believed her to be.

Dana started walking up the street, moving quickly into a section that looked unkempt compared to the buildings around the café and parlor. She had a vague idea of finding Skylar at the bar, maybe even finding out why her friend was spending so much time there.

Maybe she could even convince her that it was time to go.

I have to get out of this town.

She was so busy staring at her own feet and indulging her misery she wasn't watching where she was going. A figure swam up in her peripheral vision and she stepped aside quickly.

It was the guy who'd almost tripped her up a few days ago. "You again," she muttered, too emotionally drained for manners.

"We have to stop meeting like this," he replied, showing that strange smile of his—too toothy and faintly predatory. She didn't like his eyes. They seemed to look right through her.

She noticed with some discomfort that he had not stepped back and was still in her personal space. She took a small step back, eyeing him suspiciously. With her arms wrapped around herself and her face tear streaked, she felt exposed.

"We've got to stop meeting like this," he joked.

She didn't smile. Curiosity rose in her, as well as suspicion. Prowlers. Someone chasing her last night. Timon and his family problems. "How do you know Timon?" she demanded.

He shook his head. "We're old pals. Don't worry about that. He owes me, you see. An old debt between brothers."

"Oh, okay. Well. I guess I'll be going." She tried to sidestep him.

His face went hard immediately, the fake smile dropping like a stone.

She took another step back, starting to feel really afraid. He didn't step any closer, but she knew for a shifter, the distance between them was nothing. He could grab her and he would barely have to move his feet.

"No, you don't." His oily tone became a snarl.

"Let me past."

"No. You're snuggling up with Timon, aren't you? Oh,

you've been so careful to hide it, both of you. Never kissing, never touching. But you can't fool me."

"What?" She had no idea what he was talking about.

He laughed cruelly. "It's just the leverage I need. And here you are, walking down the street all alone. He must really think I'm a fool."

"Please, just let me by." She was starting to feel desperate. Maybe she should scream, but would anyone notice in Ragtown?

"No. I'm taking Timon's mate and I'm going to make sure he pays. He thinks he can just go and live his life like this, without a single thought for his clan? You'd think banishing him would be enough, but no. People loved his memory, the idea of him so much that it robbed me of my rightful place." He stepped towards her and she felt like he was stealing the breath from her chest.

"Please! I don't know what you're talking about!" she cried.

He snatched her arm, pulling her against him. "You will. It doesn't matter, anyway. You're just bait." He gave a nasty laugh. "Better than bait. Taking you will make him careless. I can finally get him."

"Please, no—" she tried to say.

"Just shut up." He wrapped an arm around her and started walking towards the empty lots. His grip was like steel and she couldn't pull away, no matter how hard she struggled.

"Stop it. Or I'll have to knock you out. I don't have much experience with humans, mind you, so I'll probably hit you too hard. Wouldn't want Timon to find you with a cracked skull, would we?" There was that weird, nasty laugh again.

Her heart pounded. "Timon's not my mate," she yelled. "You're making a big mistake!"

"Now, that's not true. A bear knows his brother's mate."

"Brother?" she echoed.

He unleashed a deranged cackle. "How rude of me. I haven't introduced myself, have I? I'm Vaughn, Timon's brother."

She gasped. *This evil man was Timon's own flesh and blood?*

Suddenly, things were starting to make a lot of sense.

CHAPTER 16

Timon

*L*ate in the afternoon, there was a break in customers. Timon took a breath, knowing the place would pick up again soon. But as soon as his mind was quiet, Dana filled his thoughts again. He had distracted himself all day but really, he felt awful. He couldn't believe he'd upset her like that. The thing was, he was as good as a trapped animal right now. No matter which way he went, he was going to hurt her. It just couldn't be avoided.

Still, when he heard the door, he looked up quickly, hoping it was her.

But it was Skylar and Piper.

"Hey, did you find that thing you were looking for?" He caught his sisters' eye.

"No, I did not." Piper sat at the counter, folding her

ARIANA HAWKES

hands. The look she gave him was full of anticipation, as if she was hoping for him to have news.

He turned to Skylar, who was diving into the breadbasket on the counter.

"Where's Dana?"

Skylar blinked, a hunk of bread halfway to her mouth. "She's not with you?"

A cold trickle of panic flowed through him.

When did you last see her?" Piper asked him.

"She left here. Ages ago. Before the lunch rush." His throat was tight.

He met Piper's gaze, his growing fear reflected in her eyes. "You sure you didn't find that thing you were looking for?"

"No."

"What thing?" Skylar demanded. "You guys are so cryptic. It's weird."

Piper's golden-brown eyes narrowed, silently asking him how much they should share with Skylar.

"Guys. What's going on? This is more than weird now." Skylar glared at them alternately, cocking an eyebrow.

Piper sighed and turned to her. "Skylar, I need you to trust us, okay?"

"Is Dana in trouble? Where is she?" Skylar leapt off her stool with enough force to send the breadbasket rolling down the counter, scattering crumbs.

"You two have been double weird since last night! You tell me what the hell is going on and where Dana is right now!" She stomped her foot.

"It's okay. We're going to find her," Piper said. "We have some family members hanging around that have business with Timon. They might have... wanted to talk to Dana."

"She'll be fine. No one's going to hurt her." Timon tried to

106

sound cheerful and comforting, but his bear was raging inside him. Instinctively, he knew this had gone bad. Vaughn had her and there was no doubt.

Skylar kept scowling at Timon. "Florence told me Dana was upset. She told me she sent her to talk to you because she was crying. This is all your fault!" She fired the words at him as if they were arrows.

"Skylar—"

"No! Shut up! You don't even care! You don't want a mate. Well, consider those out there who want one but can't find one. Do you have any idea how lonely it is, how soul crushing, to find out that you won't get that special someone? Especially when I look around me and you and Dana are just screwing around, not giving a crap about the gift the rest of us want so badly!"

She sniffed and rubbed her nose. "She likes you, you know. She told me this morning. She's got her own past to deal with. It's not easy for her. But she decided you were worth a try. Looks like she was wrong."

Timon was so shocked that he didn't know what to say. The news hit him with the force of an icy blast.

"Now she's gone," Skylar continued, jabbing a finger at him. "Mixed up in all your shifter crap. And she doesn't even know that you love her!"

Love her. Timon swallowed hard. She was right. He had sent Dana away, let her go without even telling her what he felt. No wonder she'd left crying. She would have been such an easy target for Vaughn, he realized and he felt sick at the thought.

"Skylar, I want you to stay with Florence."

"No, I'm helping."

"You are not!" he roared, his bear taking control. They were running out of time. Dana was out there, in Vaughn's grasp. His bear knew it, even if the human part of him kept imagining her at home watching TV.

"You will go to Florence, right now. You will not go to the saloon—or Brock's, or wherever. You will not go near the house. You will go to Florence and stay there where you are safe."

Skylar rolled her eyes, turning towards the door. "Look who finally grew a backbone."

He clenched his fists, trying to keep his bear inside him.

"What do you want to do, Timon?" Piper looked up at him, eyes wide and anxious.

"Go check the house. She might be there. Just check it out. I'll head to the woods."

"That's a pretty big space. They could be anywhere."

"Yeah, but I found him pretty easy before. Something tells me he's not going to be hiding. He wants me to see." Timon relaxed his hands, feeling his bear rising, ready to run, rip, claw and fight.

Piper gulped. "You seem to know him pretty well. That sounds exactly like what he would do."

Timon shrugged. "All I had to do was meet him once. I knew what type of guy he was."

"So why didn't you just rip his throat out! You had the perfect opportunity and you left him alive!"

"Piper, anyone can change. Anyone. Ragtown is proof of that. I had to give him a chance. If he said he didn't want to kill me, I needed to give him that option. I couldn't just tear him apart in cold blood."

She got up, staring at him defiantly. "You should have. You think you know him, great. But I've seen him in action." Her lip trembled and she ran back to the counter, throwing her arms around him. She squeezed him with all of her bear strength, until she took his breath away.

"Be careful, brother. I came here to save you, not get you killed."

"I know. Let's get out of here."

He rushed around, closing up the shop. A few disappointed customers hung around the front, but he waved them off. He saw Piper go bounding down the street, already starting to shift, to benefit from her bear's heightened senses.

Timon headed towards the woods, nose high. There was Vaughn's scent, right at the edge of the forest. He picked it up even without shifting. Right underneath it, like a haunting song, was Dana.

His blood ran cold. There was only one reason Vaughn would leave himself exposed this way.

It was a trap.

Timon shifted, and charged into the trees. His roar shook the forest as he pounded through the damp undergrowth. He absorbed the forest, he was part of it. The savage nature of his animal rode him, then overwhelmed him. Red rage poured through his vision as he raced after the scent, adrenaline pulsing through every cell.

He couldn't believe he had even tried to give his brother a chance. He would end this now, once and for all.

CHAPTER 17

Dana

*D*ana knew she was in the forest. Vaughn had blindfolded and gagged her pretty quickly, realizing that she wasn't going to stop struggling or trying to scream, but her nose picked up the rich, resinous scent of the pine trees.

Most of the trip was a blur to her. He had thrown her over his shoulder and moved quickly until the sounds of Ragtown became faint. At first, the noise of birds and wind in the trees was soothing, until she realized just how far they had come from civilization.

Would Timon find her? She knew he had excellent senses, but she didn't know if Vaughn had covered his tracks or not. When he finally pulled the rag off her face and tied her hands roughly behind her back, she saw by the closely-packed trees that they were very deep in the forest.

She was beyond crying now. All the tears of recent days had drained her dry, leaving her with a sort of dead calm. She glared at Vaughn as he paced back and forth in front of her. He dripped menace, his every glance threatening. Even though his lips were bent into a smile, there was nothing friendly in it.

"Scream if you want little missy," he sneered. "No one can hear you out here, except for a few shifters. They'd have to be in the forest, too. We're too far from Ragtown." He grinned as he stopped in front of her.

She stared back, refusing to make a sound.

"Come on, girl. Call your lover. Tell him exactly where we are."

She shook her head slowly, staring him down. Anger was rising in her, becoming stronger than fear. If she got the opportunity, she would tear his face off with her nails.

"Ohhh…going to stay quiet, are you?" Vaughn reached out to pat her hair and she recoiled violently, knocking into the tree trunk behind her. He laughed.

"Well, I guess I'll talk then. You should know exactly what you've gotten yourself into." He stroked his chin as he looked around at the trees, as if seeking inspiration.

"Timon is such bad news, our father sent him from the clan as a baby. Can you imagine that? Even from that tender age, our father knew that he was going to bring us bad luck. Anything with eyes like that is going to be trouble, you know?"

Dana set her jaw, unable to believe what she was hearing. *They kicked him out as a baby?*

"He left him out in the cold, apparently. So disgusted that he couldn't even end the little bastard's life himself. He left him for the wolves, or maybe the cold if the wild things didn't tear him to shreds first."

He paced back and forth again and Dana could hardly keep quiet. She wanted to scream at him—ask what kind of monster would abandon a child to die.

"I was already on the way, apparently. So, father knew he had an ace up his sleeve. He hoped the next son would be made of the right stuff. As you can see, I am. I'm strong. Brutal. I kill at will. And check out my eyes." He gestured at his face with a grand flourish and leaned in close, so Dana could see his brown eyes, glinting gold. They were so much like Piper's that Dana was disturbed. Familiar, but horribly wrong at the same time. Two creatures so vastly different should not have the same eyes.

"The trouble is, Timon didn't die. If he had died before I was born, natural selection would have gifted me the power of the alpha." He shook his head angrily.

"But the bastard didn't die!" His eyes glowed with fury and Dana thought he might be about to shift. Instead, he just flung his hands out, balling them into fists.

"He fucking lived. Some village woman took him on. Then she let him go. He disappeared into the world, a woeful creature, something that would only bring bad luck to everything he touched."

Dana felt cold and sick inside. She could understand now why Timon was so withdrawn, why he couldn't trust anyone. He had never had a home, never had any kind of consistency in his life at all.

Her heart went out to him as she saw him in an entirely different light. He was suffering, far worse than she was. Yes, her home had been broken. But at least she had one. She may not have ever seen her mother again, but she had a loving father who was there for her every day.

Timon had never had anyone.

"You turning up right when you did was gold. I tracked

Piper, you see. I knew the little snitch would find him. She's had an obsession with the 'lost alpha', promising the clan that he'd return. I didn't even know where to start looking, but she did. She told the clan she could stop the fighting, return our true alpha to us. She was really just being sentimental." He laughed as he stopped in front of her, swinging his left leg back and forth, as if he was thinking about kicking her. Then he shook his head in disgust.

"When she started living with him, I kept a close eye on them. I was going to use her for leverage, but I couldn't be sure he cared enough about her. A screwy-eyed bastard like that probably wouldn't care about his sister. She's also a dangerous little bear when she gets going. It could have gotten messy."

He bent down, looking right into Dana's face. Their eyes were so close together, all she could see was the darkness of his pupils rimmed with gold.

"Then you come along. A perfect, pretty, tasty treat. I suspected what was going on. I could tell by the smell you were linked together." He touched her face. "You hid it well. But not well enough. I knew that you were bound." He gave a smile of great satisfaction.

"Now I've got you, I'll be able to control him. He'll do anything for his mate. You'll see."

Dana laughed at him. She had finally found her voice and the first sound she made was a great peal of laughter.

"He doesn't even like me. He pushed me away. Why do you think I was walking down the street crying?"

Vaughn waved a hand, stepping away from her. "It doesn't matter. He'll come. I know he will. You don't get how this works if you think he can ignore his mate being in danger."

Dana frowned. Even if Timon cared enough to come and take on Vaughn, he would still have to worry about the rest of the clan, especially his father. How many fights would he have to go through before he could be free?

She drew in a trembling breath, only half-listening to Vaughn as he went on about his quest for revenge and how he had never measured up to Timon. She wanted to mention his inferiority complex but thought better of it. Better not to joke with the vicious kidnapper.

She was terrified of Timon showing up. She couldn't see any other bears, but she sensed that Vaughn wasn't here by himself. It was a no-win no matter how it went.

But through all of that, she just wanted to see Timon again. She wanted to hold him and give him her love. She knew she could heal him, if they could just have the time together.

From the look of Vaughn, they were not going to get that time. She wriggled against her ropes, but it was no good, she was tied tight. Her thoughts ran around on an endless carousel.

Wanting Timon to come, and quickly.

Wanting him to stay away and keep himself safe.

CHAPTER 18

Timon

With every step that Timon took, Dana's scent got stronger. He could tell, even from this distance, that it was rich with her pumping blood and sweet breath.

She's alive.

No single thought in his entire life had ever been as comforting as that one. He knew she was waiting for him, just as he had always been waiting for her. He was crippled with guilt at the way he'd treated her, but he tried to push those feelings away. To save her, he was going to need every scrap of confidence he had.

He plunged his nose into the soil, inhaling her scent. They were not far away now.

Off to his side, he picked up a faint sound of crunching twigs, and he whirled to face it. As he got ready to attack, a shadowy bear form collapsed in on itself and resolved into the shape of Piper, walking forward with a finger on her lips.

"They're in that clearing up ahead. Were you really just going to go running in there like that?"

He went up on his back legs and shifted fast. "Do you have a better suggestion?" he said.

"Distract him for me. I'll get Dana out. Just keep him talking."

He shook his head. "I don't like this."

"Join the club, brother. Wait for me to get Dana out of the way. Don't attack him until she's safe. Then I can help you."

"I'll deal with him by myself," he growled.

"Timon, no! You could get killed."

"All I'm worried about is you and Dana. My life isn't worth that much."

Piper stepped forward, her gaze sharp in the darkening night.

"Don't you dare say that! That's the bullshit I had to listen to growing up. That you're worthless. Well, I know now it's not true. You're kind and gentle. You notice other people and you care for them. You also make really damn good pizza!"

He grinned in spite of the situation.

"Okay, I'll be careful. For the sake of pizza," he said solemnly.

She giggled and shoved him, and he shoved her back, both of them seeming to need a moment of levity to get their confidence up.

"For Dana, you moron. She'll be devastated if she loses you."

"I don't know about that." The good mood dropped away as quickly as it had come.

"Know it, brother." Piper gave him a quick kiss on the cheek then snuck off into the shadows.

Timon prepared to face off against his brother. He could see a patch of flickering orange light where Vaughn had just lit a small fire. He really didn't care about being seen. Timon understood this was a trap, but he couldn't see how it worked. If Vaughn was just sitting there alone with Dana, he either underestimated Timon's strength or his feelings for his mate.

He looked closely to see if Vaughn had a gun. He didn't appear to have anything except his own two hands and Timon found this even more suspicious. He was pacing back and forth in front of Dana, gesturing and talking in a lofty voice.

Show pony, he thought darkly.

He hoped Piper was in position. He started to move through the trees, making plenty of noise. Vaughn turned towards him, keeping Dana behind him. Timon made a little more noise, taking his time. The anticipation drew Vaughn further up the clearing.

"Come out, you bastard! I know you're there. Doing a shitty job of sneaking up on me, too."

Timon managed to look defeated as he came out of the trees. He didn't think his brother was going to be stupid enough to fall for being played like that, but maybe Vaughn was all show and no substance.

Just keep him busy.

"I'm here, Vaughn. Just let her go now and we can settle this."

Vaughn started to laugh, holding onto his guts. "Let her go? Oh, wow. You have some funny ideas about how this works." He took a step closer and Timon was desperate to glance across the clearing to see if Piper had reached Dana yet, but he daren't take his eyes off Vaughn for a second.

"How does it work then? I thought you just wanted my

head. Now that I'm here, just let Dana go and you can have it."

"You don't understand, brother. I want your head, but once that's done, I think I'll tear up your mate, too."

Timon's bear roared inside him, so fiercely that he could barely keep it in. Vaughn didn't know what it was to be mated. He had no idea of the bond and how the bear would defend it.

"Where's that little bitch, Piper? I can only get a hint with my human nose, but she's around, isn't she?"

He turned his head and Timon took a quick step forward.

"You came for me! You better not turn your back to me Vaughn, not unless you want me to tear your spine out!"

Vaughn turned back to him and stepped up even closer. "There's a bit of fire in you, after all. I tell you, after watching you for a while, I thought you were going to be a piece of cake to take out. You seem so mild mannered, brother. I didn't think you had it in you."

"You have no idea what's in me." Timon's bear growled in his throat, his hands curling into fists. He couldn't hold back anymore. The change was streaking through his every cell. It was as if all those years of loneliness had come together inside him, finally turning on their true target.

"Not a leader, that's for damn sure. I should have had the power of the alpha, me! The clan wouldn't dare go against me then."

"What exactly do they fight you for?" Timon was still just trying to stall, not daring to look behind in case he drew Vaughn's eye. He had to give Piper enough time.

"Bears want their own territory. They want to expand it. They also want to have trades, resources. That's fine of course, but only if they pay a percentage to their alpha."

"That sounds like slavery."

"It is the leaders who are slaves, brother. We keep them safe. Half of their goods and land is barely enough to pay us back for everything we do for them."

"Half?"

"Well. Sometimes more than that, in a good year."

"You're a monster! I'm ashamed to be your blood! What the hell is wrong with you?"

Vaughn hardly reacted, smiling at Timon with a cold gaze.

"It's what's wrong with you, brother. Those crazy eyes. Nature granted you the alpha's power. But she screwed up, didn't she? You're a weakling. Not fit for the responsibility. I've got to kill you. Then I can finally have the power I deserve."

Timon grinned. He didn't know a whole lot about this, but he knew that Vaughn could never obtain the alpha's power. "Are we going to do this? Or do you just like to talk?" he asked calmly, even though his bear was raging.

Vaughn screamed, a terrible sound. His eyes went dark and the change came over him. His clenched fists burst into huge claws as the dark fur rippled across his forearms and his face twisted. The roar continued on through the change until it was the bear roaring with the might of an apex predator claiming his territory.

Timon closed his eyes and let the bear slip over him as if he was going under dark water. He and his bear had often been at odds. The bear drove him to the woods to live wild when the frustration and loneliness of trying to be around human beings became too much. Both of them had struggled with Ragtown. Timon had never known that he was an alpha.

Now he did.

He and his bear were in perfect harmony.

The change swallowed him, completely encompassing and intense. It had never felt like this before. As his eyes opened again, Timon felt the same. But he towered over Vaughn now. His bear shape was bigger and stronger than it had ever been. Vaughn roared at him, swiping at the ground. Timon planted all four feet and let out a roar like nothing he had ever heard.

Years of loneliness and confusion. The horrible isolation. Terror of being alone, forever and ever. Never staying in one place. Never having anyone care for him. Changing faces.

Piper. Dana.

Innocent bears his brother was determined to hurt. *His clan. His family.*

Dana.

Dana.

Dana.

Never alone again.

The power of the alpha flooded through him like liquid gold. With the fierce confidence that comes from being at peace with oneself and accepting of their circumstances, Timon leapt into the fight.

CHAPTER 19

Piper

*P*iper untied Dana's hands just as Timon and Vaughn rushed each other. She tried to shove Dana into the trees, but she wouldn't go.

"Get out of here! I have to help him," Piper hissed.

Dana shook her head violently. "No, Piper. I can't leave until I know he's okay."

"And we can't fight while we're worried about you getting hurt!" Piper's voice was rough as she tried to hold back her bear.

"I'm not going anywhere." Dana's eyes were huge, but steady with determination.

The fighting of the two brothers made brutal, ugly sounds—thuds of bone against bone, ripping noises from torn flesh and awful roars and bellows.

Piper looked from her brothers to Dana, hopelessly torn.

"He's the true alpha. He can win. I can't just leave you and I can't leave him."

Dana found Piper's hand and squeezed it. "I'm fine here. Just concentrate on Timon, please."

Their eyes were quickly drawn back to the fight.

The bears danced around each other, swiping and bellowing, flashing their gigantic incisors. They twisted and jumped, trying to get at each other's throats. With a mighty roar, Timon charged into his brother, knocking him off his feet. Vaughn rolled away as Timon crashed to the ground, ready to crush him. Then he bounced up and met him with razor-sharp claws. Timon let out a yelp as the honed edges swiped him across his exposed chest. Vaughn pressed his advantage, slashing and roaring.

Timon backed up, bleeding heavily and trying to get his paws up so he could block him. Vaughn kept up the onslaught, no doubt aware that if he faltered for a second, Timon would have him.

Suddenly, Timon rolled backwards, flipping to come up out of Vaughn's reach. But Vaughn dove in from the side and slammed his shoulder into Timon's, sending him flying. As Timon fell hard against a tree trunk, he let out a terrible cry.

The trees around them began to rustle.

Piper gripped Dana's hand even tighter, pressing them both closer into the tree trunk.

Roars split the air all around the clearing and Vaughn laughed crazily.

Bears began to appear among the trees. Piper gasped, recognizing them as Vaughn's faithful—those who had been promised rewards once he was alpha. They had been waiting for this moment, when Timon was tired and injured, so they could take him out.

Timon lowered his head, huffing. Then he stood up high

on to his back legs, towering over every bear in the circle. He roared at the sky in challenge and in glorious confidence.

He was the alpha. Their true leader.

The other bears rushed in and the girls lost sight of Timon. Dana tried to go after them, but Piper held her back, worried enough to join the fight but not willing to leave Dana vulnerable.

The other bears had closed into a tight circle.

"They're killing him! We have to help. We can't let him die!" Dana screamed.

Piper was stricken. She couldn't let Timon die, but Dana was going to get ripped to shreds if she left her. Timon would never forgive her if his mate got hurt.

Dana pulled away from Piper, running towards the fight. Piper leapt up after her, but the smaller woman had the advantage of surprise. She rushed to the fire, grabbed a huge, flaming branch, and laid into the nearest bear, smacking it across its back.

The bear howled as its fur caught fire, and it rolled away. Before Piper could reach her, Dana had given the same treatment to every bear she could reach.

The circle opened up. And Timon came into view, badly bloodied and struggling to get to his feet. Piper knew they had only moments before the circle closed around them again. Impulsively, she grabbed Dana's hand and they rushed over to him.

Timon's human face flickered into view as he tried to talk through his bear snout. "Run, Dana. Go. I can die happy if I know you live," he begged.

"You're not going to die!" she screamed.

"Watch out," Piper muttered. Dana looked up to see the other bears closing in again.

"Go! You have to go," Timon roared.

"I am not leaving your side," she insisted.

"It's too late, brother," Piper cut in. "They're too close. They'll kill her, too. Vaughn will go for her immediately."

Timon groaned, a sound of such despair it broke her heart. She slapped at him uselessly, begging him to get up. "There is one way," she whispered, keeping one eye on the advancing bears.

Timon shook his head, forcing himself to his feet at last. "No. Not that."

"What is it?" Dana demanded. "I'll do anything to save him, you know that."

"It will save you, too," Piper told her. "I can't see any other way out of this."

"Tell me!"

"I can turn you. I have that power. I can make you a bear."

"Make me a shifter?" Dana's voice trembled.

"Yes. You can help us and get out of here in one piece."

"I'll do it," Dana said at the exact same time Timon said, "absolutely not."

"I said I'll do it. Do it now!" Dana yelled.

"I can't let you do this," Timon insisted. "You can't become something you hate for me. I won't let you."

Dana leaned down and put her hands on either side of his big, grizzly head. She kissed his bear nose.

"I would rather live as something I hate than lose you. But how can I hate shifters, when I love both of you?" She closed her eyes, pressing her cheek to his furry snout.

Timon's eyes were full of denial, but she turned away from him, holding out her arm.

"Piper, do it, quick!"

Piper turned and gripped Dana's forearm with her teeth.

Just then a mighty roar sounded behind her. She froze, waiting for sharp nails to rip through her hide.

But nothing happened. She dropped Dana's forearm and turned her head. There was a huge brown grizzly behind her. Jagger. She picked up his bear scent immediately and relief flooded her veins. He tilted his head to the side and she knew what she had to do. She grabbed Dana by the back of her shirt and hauled her away from the circle. Immediately, half a dozen other shifters poured in, massive and bristling.

Ragtown had come to protect Timon.

Piper deposited Dana behind a tree and hunkered down breathlessly.

"D-did you do it?" Dana said in a panicked tone, rubbing at her arm.

"No, thank goodness." Piper hugged her hard.

"But I was ready."

"I know you were. And so does Timon."

As they watched, the Ragtown bears piled into the fight. They attacked Vaughn's crew hard, mercilessly, punishing them for hurting one of their own. In the midst of them was Timon, re-energized by their support. He rose up on his back legs, the tallest of all of them, and let out an almighty bellow. Then he went after Vaughn.

The two of them met in a clash of muscle and fur. At first, they seemed evenly matched, dealing vicious blows, one after another. But before long, Vaughn crashed down under the onslaught of Timon's paws. He couldn't get up; the bigger, older bear was too much for him.

Piper waited breathlessly for the mortal wound, the moment when Timon would kill their brother to save them both.

Timon took several steps back, muzzle bloodied. As one, the bears stopped fighting and looked over expectantly. Piper shuffled to the side and craned her neck.

There was Vaughn, in an ignominious heap on the

ground. Even from a distance, his fur seemed soaked, like he was bleeding out. Her heart clenched. He hadn't been a good man, and he'd tried to kill Timon—the best man she'd ever known. But he was still her brother.

His body twitched. She gasped—he was alive. Timon stepped farther back, allowing him the space to get to his feet. And slowly, slowly, Vaughn dragged himself from the clearing, half on his belly, like a snake that had been run over by a truck.

* * *

Dana

DANA RUSHED to Timon and flung herself into his arms. His fur was bristly and sticky with blood, but he shifted immediately, and suddenly he was Timon again, his kind, blue and black eyes looking into hers with deep concern.

"Are you okay?" he asked.

"Of course I am." She smiled through her tears.

He frowned. "You didn't...I mean, Piper didn't change you?"

"No. Jagger arrived and my services were no longer required."

"Thank goodness." He flung his arms around her.

"Hey, it wouldn't have been so bad being a bear, you know?" she mumbled into the side of his neck.

"But you're perfect as a human, Dana. I don't want you to change a thing." He drew back and looked at her again. "But the fact you were willing to get turned for me...that means more than I can say." His voice cracked with emotion, and she lifted her hand and stroked his beard scruff.

"I would have happily done that for you, Timon," she whispered. "And more. You're my mate."

"I am?" Despite everything, he still looked adorably doubtful.

"Of course." She pulled him close and for the second time ever, they kissed, long and deep. Love and relief flooded through her body.

WHEN THEY FINALLY DREW APART, the other guys came over, shifting into their human forms. There was Jagger, of course; Aidan, Garrett, Nikita, Rowan, Ryker, Brock, and several bears she didn't know. Most of them were injured and Dana exclaimed at the sight of all the blood.

"It's not as bad as it looks," Timon muttered into her hair. "Shifters heal fast."

"How about giving us a heads-up next time you decide to take on a whole clan by yourself?" Jagger said good-naturedly.

Timon grinned. "Sure thing. But how did you guys get here so fast?"

"We've been keeping an eye out," Jagger said. "Figured your clan was on your tail."

Timon snorted. "They're no clan of mine. But where are they?"

"They took off after their ring leader. Don't think they'll bother you again. Kind of curious to know what they want with you, though."

Timon eased Dana off his lap and she helped him get to his feet. "I'll tell you the full story on the way home. Think I've been keeping secrets from you all for long enough."

. . .

WHEN THEY ARRIVED BACK at Timon's house Piper immediately announced she needed cake and was going to head to the café.

"Where's Skylar?" Dana asked absently, running her hands through her hair and discovering it was full of leaves.

"I left her in Florence's capable hands." Piper winked at them. "I won't be back any time soon. Catch you kids later."

DANA AND TIMON waved good bye then grinned at each other.

"So sweet of her," she said.

"Yup. That's my sister." Timon bent and brushed his lips with hers. "She knows what I need, even when I'm too stupid to realize it myself." He sighed, laying his hands on her shoulders. "I'm so sorry about before. I've never belonged anywhere—never had anyone I could trust. I just pushed you away because I thought I wasn't worthy of you."

"Timon. I know. Vaughn told me. But let me tell you, I've never belonged anywhere either." She kissed him, hard and deep.

When they pulled apart for a breath, she whispered against his lips. "We belong together."

He looked at her searchingly, and in that moment, both his eyes seemed equally dark and stormy. "It's time I made you mine. But first I need a bath."

She pursed her lips. "Can I come, too?"

With a grin, he swept her up into his arms.

. . .

IN THE BATHROOM, Timon turned the faucet on full, and soon the bathtub was full of hot, steamy water. As he stripped off his pants, Dana was suddenly overcome with shyness and didn't know where to look. She kept her eyes averted as he climbed into the tub, creating a tidal wave of water with his huge bulk.

When she looked at him again, he was regarding her expectantly. Her hands went to the buttons on her blouse, but they trembled and she struggled to unfasten them.

His heavy brow creased. "What's wrong, sweet Dana?" he murmured.

"Oh...I—" She gestured at herself helplessly.

His frown deepened, then, slowly a look of under-standing came into his eyes. "Humans don't like being naked in front of each other," he said, in the tone of someone reciting something they'd learned.

It was so adorable coming from him that she giggled. "Well, *most of us* don't like getting naked in front of strangers," she said.

"But I'm not a stranger, Dana."

"I know." He did have a point, she conceded. And why *was* she shy about this man that she desired so much seeing her naked? Suddenly she felt so ridiculous that she burst out laughing. He laughed too.

"Come here," he murmured, and with his wet hands he unfastened her blouse, then her pants, and before she knew it, she was stripping off her underwear and joining him in the blissfully hot water, and she wasn't embarrassed anymore. He held her in his big arms, turned sideways on his lap, and he kissed her tenderly.

Dana melted in his embrace, all the worry and fear of the day falling away, until all she was aware of was him.

Their kisses were gentle at first, but soon they got more

and more heated, and she felt him, hard beneath her thigh. His desire for her drove her own arousal, and even beneath the water, she could tell that she was wet. Hesitantly, she reached for him, wrapping her hand around his thick erection.

He gave a low growl of need, and he grasped her hips and flipped her around until she was astride him. Her breasts were now at the height of his face, and he took one of her aching nipples into his mouth. The sensation of his tongue on her was electric, and she began to grind against him, eager to have him inside her.

Keeping his mouth right where it was, he reached down and guided himself in. He was big, filling her all the way up. The moment her insides gripped him they both moaned. Dana leaned back to give him a better angle and he thrust forward, driving into her to make them one. The hot water swirled around, making their skin slick as they slid together.

"You feel so good in my arms," he murmured as he thrust into her, looking up at her adoringly, and her heart swelled with love for her big, sexy bear.

His rhythm got faster and faster, setting her body on fire, until suddenly he leaned forward, pulling Dana back up to him.

"Only one thing's missing, then we are truly one," he muttered, his voice rough and growly.

"The mate mark," she whispered. He nodded, his different-colored eyes more intense than ever.

He drew her close, until his mouth was over the spot between her neck and her shoulder.

She stilled, trembling a little as he put his lips against her skin. When his canines grazed her, she cried out. It was like fire and ice… But it only lasted a second.

He took a firmer grip on her hips and she clung onto him,

as his thrusting went out of control. Over and over, he pounded into her, and the tension in her body built and built.

Until suddenly, a powerful orgasm ripped through her. Her body filled with swirling, crackling threads of ecstasy. A moment later, Timon unleashed a roar and he came inside her.

He held her tight until it subsided, leaving her collapsed on his shoulder.

"Now I'm truly yours," she murmured when she was capable of speech.

"Forever," he murmured with a sigh of satisfaction.

"Forever."

Then he started to rock back and forth very gently, still long and hard inside her.

Dana grinned with delight as her body came alive again under his attention. The pressure and intensity began to build again, and she knew that orgasm had been the first of many.

CHAPTER 20

Timon

As Dana writhed in his arms like a water nymph, Timon watched her in wonder. He felt like the two of them were isolated in their own little world, like a magic bubble where only they existed in the universe.

Her gorgeous body curved away from him, exposing her small, firm breasts with their sweet dark nipples. He pulled her back towards him and ran his mouth over her smooth skin, slipping her nipple into his mouth to nibble on it gently.

She moaned, tangling her fingers in his hair, and he suddenly decided it was time they got out of the water and went to bed. He reached over and turned off the faucet, then picked her up and carried her to the bedroom.

When he laid her on the bed, she stretched out, looking up at him with love. Her body was pale against the dark sheets and her skin was soft against his hard hands. He couldn't stop staring at her, trying to imprint every inch of her luscious form into his memory.

"I'm not going anywhere, Timon. It's you and me, for always," she murmured, as if picking up on his thoughts.

He lay down beside her, putting his body against hers. When they kissed it was like something inside him breaking, all those years of fear and solitude that were now being undone.

"Dana," he whispered, saying her name like a spell. He was enchanted. He could never have imagined being so whole.

She wriggled under him, spreading her legs either side of his body. He grinned and changed position to give her what she wanted, his cock still long and thick, ready to pleasure her.

She threw her head back and moaned as he started to thrust inside her. She was so small and delicate but as soon as she became intoxicated by his touch, it was like she was invincible, a creature of lust and flame. He held himself up on his arms so he could watch her buck and writhe, his cock getting harder by the second.

She responded to his every movement, clawing at his shoulders, gripping him to thrust her hips even harder against his hard cock.

He slowed down, gently caressing her breasts, and he felt his cock swell until there was no room left to thrust. She looked up at him with wide eyes, reaching up to stroke his cheek with her knuckles.

"I love you," she whispered.

A growl rose in his chest, some emotion that was as intense as fear but filled him with peace instead of uncertainty. For a moment the words swelled inside him, almost too big to be spoken at all.

"I love you," he whispered. Her face broke into an incredible smile and all he could do was lean close and kiss her.

While his tongue searched deep into her mouth, he felt her open to him completely. Head back and lips parted, she thrust her hips down and opened her thighs to him.

She was his.

He broke off the kiss, a cry like a roar pouring out of him as he began to move again. He could feel her fingers tight on his shoulders, her legs against his hips and her soft words urging him on. The wave took him over, obliterating sight and sound and leaving Dana, only Dana and the sensation of her wrapped around him.

He fell down beside her, and pulled her into his arms. He couldn't open his eyes, but her scent was all around him, her body pressed against his. He heard her breathing slow down immediately and his bear made one final grumble of pleasure before it took him into sleep.

* * *

THE WARMTH of the room woke them gently, as if the sun was caressing them into wakefulness. At first, Timon couldn't believe what his senses were telling him. Last night had been a dream. Surely it was only a fantasy that his tired mind had put together, something that he wanted so desperately he had created for himself.

But when Dana wriggled against him and kissed him, he knew it was real. Emotion swept through him as his human half tried to speak, tried to explain it or express it. His bear rumbled at him to be still, to enjoy the moment.

She kissed him again, wriggling gently against him. He

held her tighter and kissed her back, that long, hard part of him telling her exactly what he wanted first thing in the morning.

"Well, good morning," she whispered, looking under the sheets.

"And to you my love." He pulled her closer ready to possess her again. She kissed him harder, running her fingers over his body.

Then her stomach growled loud enough they both heard it.

She giggled, hugging him tighter. "Are you sure I didn't get turned into a bear?" She looked down at herself as if to confirm she still had a human stomach.

"I don't think so, but to be on the safe side, I'd better get you fed." He grinned and got out of bed before throwing on a shirt and pants. "Anyways, it's a bear's duty to make sure his mate doesn't go hungry."

She smiled as she got up, too, picking one of his big shirts from the end of the bed and putting it on. It was so big it draped right down her thighs.

"Well, I won't refuse. Seeing as it's your duty and all."

He stepped over to her and clasped her around the waist, lifting her up.

"My duty, and my pleasure."

They kissed, deep and long. Within seconds Dana's stomach grumbled again. They both laughed.

"Okay, okay." He took her hand and led her downstairs.

* * *

Dana

DANA SAT at the table while Timon started the coffee and began whisking eggs. Piper stuck her head around the corner, flashing a wide-open eyeball between her fingers as she peeked.

"You guys decent in there?" she yelled.

"Get in here!" Dana laughed. Then she blushed and said hesitantly, "Sister."

Piper came running in, and threw her arms around Dana.

"I've always wanted a sister," she whispered in Dana's ear and kissed her cheek. Then Piper gave one of her trademark grins and hurried over to Timon.

"I'm helping."

"No, you're not, sit down."

"I'm helping." Piper completely ignored him as she got out some bacon.

"I can smell breakfast! You guys are all back, and you didn't even call me," a plaintive voice called from the porch.

Dana responded, "Come in, Skylar." But it was unnecessary. Her friend was already charging down the hallway.

"Missing friends, rogue bears, reports of fights—do you guys have any idea what you put me through—"

She looked Dana up and down, then looked at Timon.

"Oh. Oh! Dana!" She jumped up and down then threw herself on her friend. They shared a hug, both of them relieved that after a few days of almost total chaos, it finally looked like everything was working out.

Piper started serving up eggs then sat down with the girls.

"So, does this make all of us honorary sisters now?"

"Of course!" Skylar almost screeched. Timon rubbed his ear and Dana threw him a sympathetic look. The violently varying pitch of this woman sure took a lot of getting used to.

"It's so great, seriously! You guys were hot for each other from the beginning, weren't you? Come on, admit it." Skylar looked between Timon and Dana, leaning back in her chair.

Dana blushed, rubbing her neck absently. As her fingers moved the collar of her shirt, Skylar's eyes lit up.

"Wow! Look at that mate mark!"

Dana had already seen it in the bathroom mirror. It was dark red and purple, just a small line of delicate dots, like stars. She blushed, looking away. Skylar leaned forward and hugged her, unbalancing her chair and almost pulling them both to the floor.

"Well, I'm sorry to be the one to do this. But now that's all done, you'll have to go back to the clan," Piper said.

"What?" Dana snapped.

"Well, he's the alpha. They need him. It's all going to hell and our father needs to be stopped. That was only the first step."

Dana was quite horrified but Timon didn't seem bothered as he sat down with a massive pile of bacon and pancakes.

"We'll go back. But I'm not ruling the clan," he said, in between bites.

Dana and Piper both looked angry about different parts of the sentence.

But Timon smiled at them both calmly. "We can go back as soon as you're ready, Piper. But I'm not taking charge of the clan. You are."

Piper almost choked on her coffee. "What? I can't, I'm not chosen like you. I have no idea what I'm doing!"

"But you do. You know them. You care about them. This job was made for you."

He finished eating his food, got to his feet and left the room.

When Dana heard the front door bang, she and Piper looked at each other and shrugged.

"Just when I think that brother of mine is done surprising me," Piper said.

The three of them sat at the table, sipping their coffee, and wondering if Timon was planning to return.

TEN MINUTES LATER, he was back, lightly perspiring and with a big, old leather bound book tucked under his arm. He dumped it on the table triumphantly, unleashing a cloud of dust, then he began to leaf through.

"I spent a lot of time up in Florence's library while I was learning to read. And one day I picked up one of her big old books on shifter history, and I learned a lot of things about laws of succession, including this." He found the appropriate page and read:

"Among bear clans, the firstborn child of *each gender* is eligible to become alpha of the clan. If the eldest child is unable to become alpha for any reason, then that honor automatically passes to the eldest child of the opposite gender."

There was a trace of mischief in his smile as he turned to Piper. "That makes you alpha, my dear."

Piper's mouth opened and closed again. "N-no, because you are *able* to be alpha."

Timon's expression turned serious again as his different-colored eyes locked onto Piper's. "Piper, I was abandoned, unwanted by my own family. Lonely for so long. I'm not *able* to go back to this place that I've never known and rule over a bunch of strangers. You know that."

Piper was silent for a long time, then she exhaled slowly, staring down at the tabletop. When she looked up again her eyes were full of tears. "You're right," she said at last. "No one should ask that of you. I guess it is my job."

Skylar raised her coffee in salute. "Long live the queen!"

Piper grinned ruefully. "Ah, hell. I should have seen this coming." She picked up a fork and dug into her eggs, trying to avoid everyone's eyes while she processed the news.

For a moment, the table was quiet as everyone focused on the food. The bright feeling of the morning was still there, even though it was shadowed by a sense of trials still to come. Under the table, Timon reached for Dana's hand and warmth flooded her as he gave it a reassuring squeeze. *As long as we've got each other, everything will be fine*, he seemed to be saying. And she felt in her heart that was true.

CHAPTER 21

Dana

Behind a line of broken, blackened trees, something lumbered. The trees were not scorched or burned, but rotten-looking as though they had been poisoned from the roots. The leaves hung dark and limp, barely clinging to life. There was no ash on the ground, but the earth looked gray. Aside from the half-dead trees, there was no vegetation at all.

In a rough clearing in the midst of the trees, a few cabins were scattered. All of them were made of wood rotted to white, with broken planks and holes in the walls. No smoke rose from the chimneys, no gardens were cultivated at their sides. The cabins looked abandoned except for small points of light showing at the dingy windows.

Two bears crossed the clearing hesitantly, noses to the air. They were both dark, one night black. They moved slowly, sniffing the ground and looking up to the sky. A small human rode on the back of the larger one, clinging tight to the thick fur on the back of its neck.

As they came to the largest cabin, the biggest bear rapped on the door with its paw.

Dana slid off his back. She immediately wrapped her arms around herself, shivering at the sudden loss of body heat. Piper shifted and Dana handed her a robe from the pack she carried.

"Why is it so dark? It's only midafternoon," Dana muttered, looking at the sky.

"It's always like this." Piper's voice was dull, her eyes low. None of her usual warmth came to life in this place.

The door cracked open, and two people peeked out into the gray light. They were both thin, with sallow skin and drawn features.

Timon looked into the faces of the man and woman that he had seen before but could never have remembered.

"Who are you?" The man's voice was unsteady as his eyes darted over the large bear that darkened his door.

Timon shifted down, taking on his human form in moments. Dana passed him a robe that he threw carelessly over his shoulders, never taking his eyes off his parents. "Look me in the eye, father, and tell me you do not know me," he demanded.

His mother exclaimed, a wordless expression of surprise. She leapt forward and hugged and kissed Timon.

The man grabbed Timon's hand and shook it firmly, patting him on the shoulder with his other hand. "My son," he said, over and over again. "My son."

As they stepped back, they noticed Piper standing behind him. His mother kept smiling, but something in her eyes turned cold.

"Piper. You have been away a long time. You were not given leave to go."

Piper's head dropped, and Dana was shocked to see all of her friend's fire extinguished.

"I'm sorry mother," she muttered, but still, she did not look up.

"Well, do not keep my children and their friend on the doorstep! Come in, my son is home and so is my daughter. This is a great day!" Timon's father cried.

Timon followed them inside. Dana could see that he was wary, every line of his body was on alert, while his eyes swept back and forth, looking for a threat. Piper stood almost forlornly, all her light and vivacity gone. She looked at the dark, dreary corners of the house with obvious hatred, her expression pained and timid.

Timon's father ushered them towards a couch, so old and dusty it looked like no one had sat on it for years.

"Sit, my son, sit!" His father reached out to him but Timon pulled away. When his mother reached for him, Timon was even more reluctant. Both of his parents sat on the adjacent couch, looking at each other nervously. Timon eventually sat down at one end, Piper and Dana at the other. Dana tried to comfort Piper by holding her hand, but Piper kept her eyes down, lip trembling.

"You greet me like you missed me," Timon said at last. "Yet you sent my own brother to kill me?"

The couple looked at each other, faces pale and drawn. His mother shook her head, trying to meet Timon's eyes as she reached for his hand. Timon pulled away again, almost standing up. His parents shared another look. No matter how welcoming they seemed, Timon was not ready for affection.

"We tried to stop him, son. He went mad, wanting the

power of the alpha. Wanting to take my place. He believed the only way to do that was to kill you." His father shook his head, regret lining his face.

"He was out of his mind when he left here. He was never strong, our dear Vaughn. We tried with him, we tried everything. But he couldn't be controlled." Timon's mother made another move, as if to go to her son. But Timon gave her a firm look that kept her in her seat.

They both hung their heads in shame. Dana squeezed Piper's hand and Piper looked up at her, eyes hard and her face stern. She shook her head imperceptibly.

Something's not right.

Piper had lived with these people—and Vaughn—for her whole life. Dana could tell she was trying to warn them but was too afraid to step up and speak. What had they done to her, this sweet, affectionate girl? Had she waited her whole life to come to a place like Ragtown, where she could be social and loving? What horrific history would force her into being silent, sullen and obedient?

"We are relieved to see you well. We hoped that Vaughn would find his end with you." Timon's mother smiled, an ugly expression on thin lips with dark teeth lurking behind.

"He did not," Timon said curtly. "He's still alive. I don't know where he is."

His parents looked at each other in surprise, something passing between them.

"Tilda. Here is our long-lost boy, his wayward sister and good friend to both, sitting here without refreshment. Bring us something, please."

"Of course, Harry." Tilda stood up and headed for the kitchen.

The silence was worse than awkward. They all stared at each other, Harry maintaining his odd smile while the others continued to get more uncomfortable. Timon took a breath, face dark as a thundercloud.

Piper reached out, shaking her head *no. No. Don't ask or volunteer anything.*

Timon's eyes softened as he looked at his sister and he nodded. He would stay quiet.

Tilda returned with a large tray, balancing cups and cookies. The biscuits looked pale and dry, the tea far too strong with an oily slick on top. Tilda smiled as if it were a great delicacy, carefully placing the cups down in front of her guests.

She sat back with Harry, holding his hand. When they looked into each other's' eyes, the smile they shared was sickly-sweet.

Timon picked up his cup. "Thanks," he muttered absently.

He raised it to his lips, but at the same moment, Dana leapt up, arm darting out.

The hot liquid gushed out, splattering the table, while the cup shattered on the floor.

"It's poison!" Dana screamed.

Tilda unleashed a scream of pure rage.

Timon rose up to his full height, towering over his parents even in human shape. His eyes blazed with fury.

"How could you do this to your son?" Dana's voice cut the air like a knife. She stood next to Timon, half his size, but suddenly unafraid.

Tilda hissed, her eyes black like a snake. "He's a bad omen. From the second he was born. Demon, evil child!" She drew back her lips and spat at him.

"If we spill his blood, life will return to our land! It has been dying every day since he was born. He's evil."

There was a loud gasp. "You're evil!" screamed Piper, pushing through to stand beside Dana. "He was never evil! I tracked him down to see for myself if you really were wise soothsayers or ignorant fools! What I found was worse—you're vindictive, hateful creatures! The land was dying long before he was born. It isn't Timon's fault!"

She jabbed a finger at her mother, eyes glowing. "It's yours! You were the alpha chosen by grandfather, weren't you! Between your malice and father's greed you have destroyed the clan!"

Tilda and Harry leaned on each other, laughing.

"The poor dear is having one of her fits again. We shall have to lock her in the cellar. You spent far too much time with your mad old grandmother. I dare say, you've been infected." Tilda smiled cruelly at her daughter.

"Change. Shift now and give yourself a chance." Piper spoke each word with deep resonance, her bear growling.

"You wouldn't attack your own parents!" Tilda laid a hand on her chest, fear starting to creep into her eyes.

"Would parents kill their own children?" Timon's voice was low, but determined.

The brother and sister cast off their robes. Their bear shapes filled up the space, pushing furniture aside. Timon's parents screamed, and in another second, they'd shifted into huge, grizzled bears.

Dana barely had time to dart behind the couch as they rushed together.

The two old bears were both alphas, even if they were old and sick in the mind. It was ugly. Claws and fangs raked through flesh, and roars and grunts and bellows of pain filled the room. But Dana could see that Timon was holding back through it all. He could easily take out the older bears, but he did not want to hurt them. Her heart went out to him all over again. He was a beautiful soul trapped by torturous circumstances.

How he had survived with any heart at all was a miracle.

Suddenly, Tilda darted away from the others and went directly for Dana. As two rows of gnashing, yellow teeth swam into her vision, she screamed.

Then there was an almighty roar, which Dana knew was Timon's. She screwed her eyes closed, praying he'd get to her in time.

At that moment, a side door blasted open. The cold wind screeched through the room as another bear charged in. While Tilda's attention was distracted, Dana crawled frantically to the other side of the room.

Huddling beneath the smaller sofa, she could barely see anything. As the other bear joined the fray, the fighting got too intense for the small space. Claws and teeth flashed in the shadowy dark, noises of heavy blows and the tearing of fur screamed in her brain.

Finally, Timon moved into the center of the room and shook himself. The room fell silent, and slowly, Dana dared lift her head and look around. Behind Timon were the bodies of two brown bears who did not get up.

Tilda and Harry, and they seemed to be dead.

Dana rushed to Timon, hugging him. He shifted mid hug, and their bodies came together, not caring what shape they were in. She was busy looking him over when Piper let out a roar. Her face was wild with confusion as she stood over the mystery bear.

"*You* killed them!" Piper said, shifting fast.

The bear shifted, and in its place was...Vaughn.

Dana gasped.

Vaughn's face looked different, like a man who had woken from a bad dream. "I knew I had to do it. They poisoned my mind. Piper, you know...you know how they did it. You never broke, never." He shook his head, looking at the floor to hide his tears. "You were strong. You never broke. I just did as I was told."

Piper moved over to him, and stroked his face. Despite everything, Dana's heart went out to them, the upbringing of two siblings in such horrid conditions, impossible for her to imagine.

"I'm sorry Vaughn. I know. But—"

"I know," he cut in. "You won't ever be able to trust me. I get that. But I came here to kill them."

"It's done," she said grimly.

They helped each other up, turning to Timon. Vaughn held out his hand, then thought better of it. Instead he turned his head, exposing his jugular.

"I'm yours, alpha. Do your will."

Timon had more than enough reason to kill him and by clan law, he was even expected to. Still, Timon let his hand fall. He shook his head.

"I'm not like them. I can't bring you death... Brother."

They looked into each other's eyes, and then Timon clapped him on the shoulder.

Sensing that they needed a moment together, Dana headed outside and Piper followed.

As they walked into the bare clearing, sunlight streaked through the clouds. It was pure, glittering, bright. It found Piper, dusting her light brown hair until it glowed, making her eyes glint like golden jewels.

"I've never seen sun like this here. A good omen, at last," she said and raised a hand, watching the warmth trace her skin. "And all thanks to Timon." She turned to Dana. "And to you. For giving him the love and support to become his true self."

The sound of footsteps alerted them to Timon and Vaughn appearing behind them. They looked calm. Vaughn had lost that malicious cast to his features, and he looked chastened, but kind of satisfied as well, as if he'd done something that he'd wanted to do for a long time.

Timon went to Dana and put his arm around her shoulders. She sunk into him, so proud of her brave mate. "You were so brave, baby," he murmured into her ear and shivers went through her.

"No, you were," she replied. "I know how hard that was for you. You've got the kindest heart, Timon."

Suddenly, figures began to appear in the distance. It was the clan, approaching on shuffling feet. Some came forward in human shape, others in bear form. They gathered around, looking at each other uncertainly.

When Timon stepped forward, Dana's gut tightened. He was going to announce that he would stay and lead them. And she knew already that she would stand by his side. She would go anywhere Timon was. He was her home now.

She waited. Everyone was waiting for his words.

"Meet your new alpha!" he roared, his voice shaking dead leaves from the trees.

But instead of standing in place before them, he stepped to the side and bowed his head to his sister.

Piper walked forward, each step steady as she looked over the clan. The sunlight danced in her hair as she pulled back her hood, turning to face all of them with her palms out.

Timon stepped closer to her and knelt.

One by one, the others fell to their knees and showed their throats in submission.

One of the older ones struggled to kneel down. Piper hurried to her, lifting her up.

"Do not kneel, Aunty. Your poor knees!"

"And that, my child, is why you should be alpha. You care

more about our lives than if we can bow. Your grandmother would be proud of you," the old lady said.

The rest of the bears stood, those who had been in human form all changing. Every bear in the valley turned up his voice and roared into the sky in celebration of the new queen.

EPILOGUE

*M*idday in Ragtown was as stunning as ever. Dana couldn't believe she was getting to live her life in such a beautiful place. The sky was clear and cornflower blue, the mountain peak edged with silver gray clouds. She shielded her eyes from the sun to take it all in, letting it take her breath away all over again.

"Good afternoon, Dana dear." Florence's voice startled her, and she spun around, almost falling over a big wooden sign. It read 'street party, Main Street, today!' in a great flourish of yellow.

"Oh, is that for the party?" Dana asked excitedly, seeing the massive cake in Florence's hands.

"It is. But it's chocolate. So, there might not be enough," the mischievous squirrel matchmaker said.

Savannah laughed from the doorway of the café. "I have four chocolate cakes here, guys. We also have some other flavors, if anyone's interested."

"Looks like we'd better save our appetites for later," Kelly said, as she and Aidan took a seat at an outside table.

"No chance," Aidan replied, with a typically wolfy grin.

Rowan and Jagger arrived from the opposite direction, Rowan carrying a big box of fresh produce.

"Oh! You brought it! Thank you." Dana hurried over to them.

Rowan gave her a kiss on the cheek. "Anything for you, honey."

"Let me take these inside." Dana trotted into the pizza parlor to put the fresh food out the back. Not only were they doing a whole selection of pizzas made with the local produce, Dana was starting up a new line of sandwiches. She was slow cooking meat and baking her own bread in preparation to try out her creations on the citizens of Ragtown.

By the time she got back outside, the street was filling up. Garrett had arrived with the children and they were running through the crowd, laughing and chasing each other. Jagger was sitting with Brock and Rayleigh, who'd brought a keg of their own craft beer.

Callan and April were talking with Savannah, most likely about her experience of carrying a shifter baby—Dana deduced from the way they were taking it in turns to touch April's pregnant belly.

Dana looked around, thinking that this was a conversation Skylar would want to be a part of. She looked around, but her friend was nowhere to be seen.

"Where's Skylar?" She addressed the question to no one in particular.

"She's gone to the saloon, my dear," Florence whispered in Dana's ear with a secretive face.

"Again?" She groaned. "It isn't safe."

"She's fine. Trust me, Dana. She'll come to no harm there."

Dana had a million questions, but she could tell that

Florence wasn't about to open up. Before she could think more on it, she saw her mate pushing through the crowd.

"Timon!" she yelled, running up to him and throwing herself into his arms. As they came together, the rest of the world faded away. She burrowed her face into his neck, taking a big sniff of his spicy, earthy scent before finding his lips for a kiss.

"You sniff me a lot." He laughed.

In reply she inhaled again. "Can't help it."

"I was just talking to Piper." He put her back on her feet but didn't let her go.

"How is she?" Dana leaned against his chest, still breathing him in.

"She's doing great. She's putting the clan back to rights. Everyone is more comfortable, the land is coming back to life again. It looks like they'll be able to start growing crops soon, so everyone can prosper."

"Will she come back to Ragtown?" She stayed against his chest, not wanting to lose contact with him.

"She wants to. She loved it here. It depends on whether Vaughn can lead and if the others would accept him."

"He's not an alpha," Dana said automatically.

"No. But the right can be earned."

For a few moments they stood together among the swirling chatter of their friends. The party was full of laughter and loud, companionable conversation.

Dana pulled back to look up into Timon's eyes. They both smiled at the same time, and Dana squeezing him tightly.

"Do you want to go for a run in the woods?" he whispered.

"But the party! I'm supposed to be making sandwiches, you're supposed to be making pizza—"

"Do you want to go for a run with me?" His grin was

mischievous. Lately she had seen a whole new side to her mate. He was playful, gentle... Spontaneous and fun.

"Yes!" She laughed, and they took off towards the woods. He charged after her, gaining on her. As they reached the trees, he shed his clothes and she slipped onto his back in a way that was becoming familiar. He roared and she let out a yell of pure exhilaration.

They bounded through the forest, racing among the trees, until they came to their favorite clearing. Timon shifted and they collapsed into a bed of soft, green leaves, arms wrapped around each other.

"Sometimes I wish you'd turned me that day," she murmured.

His thick eyebrows drew together. "Why?"

She gazed up at the canopy of leaves. "Just seems like a lot of fun being a bear."

He grinned. "It is. And it's even more fun being a bear with a beautiful human mate. You're perfect as you are."

"Are you sure?"

His eyes turned serious. "Of course. How can you ask?"

"I don't know. Sometimes I just think of you and Piper hanging out and play fighting, and I wonder if you'd be happier mated to another bear—" She broke off. "What I mean to say is that you can turn me if you want."

Timon gave a laugh of surprise. "You'd do that for me?"

"I'd do anything for you. You deserve it."

He shook his head. "No. Dana, I do not want you to become a bear. I want you to continue to be the smartest, toughest human I've ever met. And in time, I want us to have lots of little half human-half shifter babies. How about that?"

She gave a sigh of relief. "That sounds great."

He smiled, pulling her back down for a kiss. She wrapped

her arms around his shoulders, feeling their hearts beating together.

"But knowing you were willing to make that sacrifice for me that day—I'll never forget that, Dana. Never." He kissed her fingertips, and she snuggled closer, hands roaming across his chest.

"I thought we had a party to go to." He chuckled.

"And you said you wanted to run in the woods." Dana winked at him as she leaned down for another kiss, the feeling of her lover under her hands all she would ever need to survive.

THE END

THANK YOU!

Hi, thank you for reading Timon and Dana's story. I really hope you enjoyed it, and if so please consider leaving a review; even if it's only a line or two, it will be greatly appreciated. <3

If you haven't read the previous books in the series yet, you can get them on my website at arianahawkes.com/matematch-outcasts.

Also! In case you didn't know, I have a complete **15-book totally binge-worthy matchmaking series** available. It features Shiftr, the secret dating app that helps curvy girls and sexy shifters find their happy ever after! Many of the books have been bestsellers - and my readers tell me that Shiftr is their favourite app yet! ;-) Visit arianahawkes.com/shiftr to start your journey! :-)

If you like to be notified of new releases, sign up for my mailing list at arianahawkes.com/mailinglist. You can also follow me on BookBub at bookbub.com/authors/ariana-hawkes

Thanks again for reading – and for all your support!

Yours,
Ariana Hawkes

SHIFTR: SWIPE LEFT FOR LOVE - BOOK 1 (DINA)

The original best-selling dating app series, relaunched for summer 2020!

What if your fated mate was just an app swipe away?

Immerse yourself in the loves and adventures of sassy girls and sexy shifters as Shiftr, the **secret dating app**, helps them find their happy ever after. There are **fifteen books in the series**. Visit arianahawkes.com/shiftr to begin your exciting journey with the paw-print dating app!

★★★★★ **"Shiftr is one of my all-time favorite series**! The stories are funny, sweet, exciting, and scorching hot! And they will **keep you glued to the pages!**"

★★★★★ "**I wish I had access to this app**! Come on, someone download it for me!"

Curvy Dina hates the idea of online dating. But her best friend Lauren has a secret she's bursting to share: there are men out there who absolutely love voluptuous girls like her. All Dina has to do is tap Shiftr, the cute little paw-print app that Lauren has just installed on her phone…

Get at arianahawkes.com/shiftr

ALSO BY ARIANA HAWKES

Boreas Reborn (In Dragn Protection Book 2)

Wounded Wings (In Dragn Protection Book 3)

Broken Hill Bears

Bear In The Rough (Broken Hill Bears Book 1)

Bare Knuckle Bear (Broken Hill Bears Book 2)

Bear Cuffs (Broken Hill Bears Book 3)

Christmas Bear Shifter Romances

Winter Bearland

Hill Bear Christmas

Three Shifter Christmas

Ultimate Bear Christmas Magic Box Set

Bear All I Want For Christmas Boxed Set

Bear Home For Christmas

Bear Christmas Magic

Bear My Perfect Gift

Polar Bears' Christmas

Standalone books

Lost To The Bear

Ravished by the Ice Palace Pack

Your free book is waiting!

A 4.5-star rated, comedy romance featuring one kickass roller derby chick, two scorching-hot Alphas, and the naughty nip that changed their lives forever.

The only thing missing from Aspen Richardson's life is a man who will love her just the way she is. In the small town she calls home, bullies from the past remain, making her wonder if it's ever going to happen. But, things are about to change in a major way, as the secret Aspen's parents have been keeping from her comes out...

"This book definitely needs to be added to your MUST read list – you will quickly fall in love with this steamy and fast paced story."

Get your free book at arianahawkes.com/freebook

ABOUT THE AUTHOR

USA Today bestselling author Ariana Hawkes writes spicy romantic stories with lovable characters, plenty of suspense, and a whole lot of laughs. She told her first story at the age of four, and has been writing ever since, for both work and pleasure. She lives in Massachusetts with her husband and two huskies.

Sign up for updates at arianahawkes.com/mailinglist.

www.facebook.com/arianahawkes
www.twitter.com/arianahawkes
ariana@arianahawkes.com

Made in United States
Troutdale, OR
02/02/2024

17370250R00105